12. LYUBLYANA ATANASOVA

12.

is as unique as every callus on your hands.

She spares it a glance, a nod, and returns to her work. She passes from texture to texture, pays little attention to colour. Her eyes narrow, each hour that hangs on her lids making her squint harder. Her fingers slip, smooth over. She pricks herself on the glass pieces half a dozen times a day. There's always golden paint under her fingernails and on her pisiform bone.

By noon her stomach is making ungodly noises but her legs have gone completely numb and she is loath to move. Eventually, a pot of noodles is procured. She keeps working as she eats.

In the afternoon, the noises of the town grow lazy, sluggish and monotonous, no longer providing the refreshing soundtrack of early morning. So she puts on some music. She has a soundtrack for each month. She likes to sneak in a couple of songs about a winter wonderland in each one, except for December. December doesn't need any of that with its late sunrises, gutter-coloured days and early sunsets. December with its betrayals and disappointments that she has grown to almost look forward to in the way you look forward to finishing that last bite of the meal you didn't enjoy even one bit.

There are conversations going on in her head as she makes the figurines. She likes to think that they are talking themselves to life – her angels. But it's probably unwise to tell anyone that angels are having conversations in her head or under her guiding hands, as she moulds them carefully – one nip at a time.

Truth is, it's pretty lonely work. And when your hands are so

1.

Her Angels

A day has a finite number of minutes and an infinite number of moments – you can always find out which minute you have woken up in but you can never know which moment you have stumbled into.

She gets up at 5 am every damn morning and December is no different. The sun will raise and she must do so before it. She combs her black and silver hair and twists and turns until she is sure that it will stay out of her face until the day is through.

She sits on the floor. A desk has always felt out of place in her private space and she realized a long time ago that her waist cannot handle working at a table. She sets everything up and brews a cup of something stronger than coffee. Forms have started to emerge under her palms by the time the sun graces the sky with its presence. About time too.

People think she watches the sunrise every morning.

She does get a worrisome sense of satisfaction from destroying their romantic notions.

You get up at 5 am day after day and see how long it takes you to figure out that the sun rises each time and every sunrise occupied and your brain – quite the opposite, doesn't everyone start having conversations in their head? And it's all downhill from there. How is she to know if she is talking to herself? Or if she is talking with someone else in her head? Or if her angels are welcoming each other into the world of existence and commerce and she has just grown to understand their silent holy language?

She supposes it's all crazy talk anyway and it's not like she's particular about what kind of crazy she will be. Although, she does like the thought of her angels telling stories. Stories of the places they are about to be.

She is really enjoying the one today – about some blonde girl – twenty or so – to be engaged to some banker's son. The whole house all in a ditzy about it. Her new dress with the little pearls sown into the neckline and her mother sending her to her own hairdresser for the first time because. And the table heavy with fruits that have no business being there in the middle of December and her mother going on about too many colours and her father going on about too few chairs. And then the bell is ringing and she is not there and the door of her closet is ajar and her coat is missing. And then by Christmas one of the Dallas boys from the post office is also missing – his closet door probably hanging open and his worn gloves gone.

It's exactly the kind of story that her angels like to tell. The kind she loves to listen to. She is quite convinced their stories – real or not – keep her better company than any person could – real or not.

Her fingers clutch the little brush in her hand tighter, her eyes zero in on the little nook that she missed, her tongue peeks out as if to help direct her in her task. For a moment everything goes silent.

She used to have an imaginary friend. Not an angel but an elf. Not a dwarf either – no, an elf. She had to correct everyone all the time. He was the picture of haughtiness and mischief, not that she knew either of those words back then, but remembering him now she can tell.

She quits her work when the sun sets. She can work before it has risen but not after it is gone. In the evenings, the artificial light makes her angels seem less alive and almost grotesque in their pretence to be so. She shudders to think that's how most people see them.

She does not get up immediately. She puts all her things to the side – carefully at first, one by one: the finished pieces, the ones she will continue working on in the morning, the ones that are still rough glass. Her patience seeps out gradually until her arms sweep the supplies along the floor – like wipers across a windshield, stubbornly fighting the unceasing snow.

Next she stretches out her legs – one by one, unfolding them like ancient pieces of paper that have been stuffed in some back pocket for ages, feels them tingle in a mix of pleasure and pain – little needles erupting everywhere she is trying to move for the first time in hours. She bends her spine, tilts her head back and stares at the barely-there ceiling in the scant light coming from the large windows. Then she straightens again, takes a deep breath and drapes her whole self over one leg, then the other.

She lies there with her forehead pressed to her knee – sometimes she falls asleep like this, in this endless loop of work and sleep that is the month of December – sometimes she is not sure she has woken up at all.

At the end of the day, only her angels prove that her fingers have been to work.

The mere thought of them suddenly makes her hands throb in white hot pain and she hears her own soft moan from a distance. She sighs, she straightens, she sits, she stands, she staggers toward the small bathroom. She puts the plug in the sink, turns on the cold water and watches it fill the small space. Her own little sea of salvation. When it's mostly full, she turns off the tap and slips her hands in, sinks all the way to her elbows and soaks the sleeve that has rolled down one arm. She stands there, shoulders sagging, chin resting on her chest, for ten minutes, fifteen, maybe twenty. Her newly reawakened legs start to protest, the back she keeps perfectly straight all day while working whines and twists in the unnatural position. Her fingers tingle. They know. This won't do tonight.

She takes a deep, white bowl covered in blue snowflakes and fills it with cold water, considers, adds a few drops from a little vial above the sink. She slips beneath the cold sheets and white pillows on her bed, squeezes the bowl between her knees so it doesn't sway and spill, and carefully submerges her red and prickled fingers into the blessedly cold water. Finally, her sigh is one of contentment.

It could be any night in the whirlwind of December, it could be *the* night for all she is aware.

Her angels have taken up a song that is nothing if not out of season. She smiles and lets it lull her to sleep.

2.
New Tales From the Old Forest

Growing up in a home without books, you never realize that something is missing. You don't know about all the portals to other worlds – innocuous, straight-backed, neatly stacked on shelves, hiding in plain sight. You see the towering, sturdy bookshelves in movies and bookstores but never think they belong with you. Then you visit a friend or an aunt and you find it odd that they have so many, that's if you notice at all. You don't miss them because you don't know them. It's just one of those things that you can blame your parents for later on.

But then again, just because you meet someone for the first time later in life – it doesn't mean you will love them any less.

Her son is a reader. She is not sure how much credit she can take for that. She thinks she has raised him well, better than she expected to on her own. But there's only so much belief in magic that she can nurture and only so much love for books she can pass on. And her kid has definitely surpassed her capacity for both.

It's really no surprise that Christmas is a Big Deal™.

Part of her dreads every December 1ˢᵗ. She just knows that one morning she'll wake up and find herself on the North Pole, it's only a matter of time before Ben figures out how to get them there. So far she simply finds herself in an apartment awash with the sounds of the season's best hits. By the end of the first week of that long-awaited month she lives among dwarves and Santas of all materials and sizes, has chocolate bells and candy canes falling on her every time she reaches for the flour and is constantly illuminated in some combination of red, green and gold.

How her son developed such an affinity for the holiday with her not-quite-a-Grinch-but-definite-Scrooge-undertones attitude, she will never know. Mostly she likes to blame it on kindergarten and school teachers like Miss Blair and Mrs. Pike. If she didn't know better, she'd think them related to Santa himself.

But Ben always manages to sweep her along in his excitement and every last bit of space on the surface of their fridge – covered in drawings or photos of the two of them building snowmen, hanging lights, reading by an imaginary fireplace, decorating the Christmas tree, baking cookies and performing every other cliché in the holiday book – is a testament to that fact.

Is it really any wonder that she is willing to do almost anything to ensure that her kid has whatever his pure, believing little heart wants for Christmas?

Of course, there are some things her son has without a doubt inherited from her. Like the ability to make her life as difficult as possible.

While every kid and their nerdy-turned-awesome aunt or uncle are obsessed with superheroes and Jedi and everything to do with them, racing each other to buy comics, rubber hammers and plastic lightsabers, ordering DVDs and booking cinema tickets months in advance, Alyson Rose is standing in front of a shelf filled with luxurious, leather-bound editions of *New Tales From the Old Forest* and hoping beyond hope that David fucking Arkwright puts a new book out before Christmas starts really breathing down her neck.

"Mom! Mom, you won't believe it!"

He clambers on the bar stool at their kitchen island with all the gracelessness and speed of an excited eleven-year-old and all she can do is eye the shaking legs wearily and give him a stern look.

"Don't rock the chair, Ben."

"The chair is rocking itself. This is so big, mom!"

"Is it now?" she reaches for the oregano and listens carefully, not giving anything away until she has all the details.

Knowing her son, kind soul extraordinaire, she might accidentally adopt a family of frogs, if she isn't careful.

"Yes! I know what I want for Christmas!"

Now her ears really perk up. She turns down the heat on the stove and leans one hip on the counter, giving him her full attention.

"Has Mr. Arkwright given the tree elves crossbows in this

one?" she asks, quirking an eyebrow.

"Mom," Ben groans in undisguised embarrassment, dropping his forehead on the counter like the overdramatic little diva he is. "Tree elves have magic, they don't need crossbows. Plus, the new book doesn't come out until March."

"Then what's the big news?"

"He's coming here! He's signing in Chicago on the 21st!"

Ben's whole face is alight with joy, yet before her instinctive happiness can take over, an uneasy sense of apprehension settles over it in the pit of her stomach.

She knows how much he loves these books, knows that David Arkwright is little less than a god in the eyes of her kid. She also knows that idealizing someone never ends well. Unless they are never given the chance to disappoint you.

Never meet your heroes and all that.

So until a minute ago she was entirely content with her son having a male role model that never got the chance to let him down, hurt him or disillusion him in any way.

Now she realizes she was living under a false sense of security.

"Alright. But, Ben, it might be a private event or—"

"It's not! It's in the bookstore right across from Kari's and it's totally free and you don't even have to have a book but, of course, we do."

"Of course."

Having "a book" is a slight understatement. They have all six of Arkwright' books. In each of the three editions they've come out in.

"Just let me look into it first, ok?"

"Mom," Ben jumps off the chair and comes to stand before her so the puppy eyes are in full effect when he looks up. "This is all I want for Christmas."

It's settled. If David Arkwright disappoints her kid, she's going to kill him.

That night she sits down to investigate the author of her son's favourite book series with all the skill and more distrust than she employs for the worst cases of insurance fraud that cross her desk. To say she is in for a surprise is another understatement. David Arkwright is… not what Alyson expected from an author of fairytales, even unconventional ones.

Born in Canada. Orphaned at age 8. Lived with his aunt until she had a fatal stroke when he was 11. Tossed around group homes for the next five years. Left the foster system at 16 and got a job as a delivery boy at a flower shop. Supposedly started working on the first book of *New Tales from the Old Forest* during that time. Found a job in a bookstore. Moved to America. Worked at the Jackson Public Library for two years while writing NTOF. Published his first short story in a local newspaper at 22. Moved to Chicago at 23. Got engaged to a Miss Sawyer. Published his first NTOF book in 2010. Lost his fiancé to a drunk driver two weeks after becoming a New York Times bestselling author. Dropped off the face of the earth.

(She takes a deep breath, resurfacing from the life she plunged into. It feels a lot like floating without a compass or land in sight, pulled and pushed by forces beyond her control. She pours herself a glass of wine and gets an extra blanket before she settles back in front of her computer.)

Arkwright resurfaced a year later in Montreal. Worked at a flower farm for a year and a half. Was involved in a bar fight, prosecuted and acquitted. Shook the literary circles with the second and third NTOF books in 2013.

(Critics describe them as "two shades too dark" and she just rolls her eyes and marvels at the fact that the guy is still writing fairytales.)

Regained and solidified his bestselling status. Continued to publish a new book in the series every year, while maintaining a low public profile. Sponsored the opening of a new library in Jackson. Created a program for first time offenders at the flower farm he worked at. Did one world tour in 2015 and a dozen or so signings overall in America.

And now he is coming back to Chicago and has, completely without his knowledge, managed to keep her awake until 3 am on a week night and make her almost as excited as her son to meet him in person.

In photos he looks a little rough around more than just the edges – she might even say threatening, but he is also surprisingly soft-spoken in all the videos she finds of him at premieres and signings and Alyson decides she will just have to wait and see what he's really like for herself.

She takes the first book to work. She ignores the confused or teasing looks and eats her lunch in the company of some dwarves and a homeless boy that's anything but snow white.

She is 40 pages into the second one and thinking how badly she wants to punch an incorporeal being in his smug see-through face when smoke starts rising from the oven. She yells out that they're having pizza for dinner and makes sure to bookmark her page before she goes to put out the potential fire.

She tries to concentrate on the new episode of The Handmaid's Tale for the first 10 minutes before saying fuck it, hitting the space bar with her toe and reaching for the book that holds the fate of a pompous prince lost in a devious, living, breathing and entrapping garden and the princess that turns into a lion to save him.

On Saturday she asks Ben what he wants to do and almost fistpumps the air when he says he's invited to a sleepover. She doesn't though. She loves her kid. But she does end up buried under three blankets, gingerbread crumbs in her bed and a cup of milk on the nightstand, consuming David Arkwright' fourth book in under 6 hours. Her eyes hate her.

It snows on Sunday. Ben binges the first four Harry Potter movies. She may or may not cry her way through *New Tales from the Old Forest V*.

She closes the last book at 2 am on a Wednesday and starts for Ben's room before she remembers he has been asleep for hours. So she opens her laptop and googles all the details about David Arkwright' signing instead.

Ben is ready to start chipping away at his mom's patent "let me look into it" the very morning after he tells her about the signing. He shovels cereal into his mouth as quickly as humanly possible so they don't have to rush to school and he can have plenty of time to plead his case. Then, as he is grabbing his backpack, he sees her put the first *New Tales from the Old Forest* book in her own bag and he hesitates. He knows his mom, he knows she will cave eventually, and yet, maybe he can save himself some grovelling. He knows how great NTOF is and how awesome David Arkwright must be. Maybe she can enjoy it as well. Maybe she doesn't have to take him just because he begs it of her. Maybe she will want to go.

So Ben decides to play a long game. Well, alright, a week-long game. He can give her a week.

The next day he runs for the pizza when he hears the doorbell and doesn't fail to spot the next book on the sofa, his mom's frayed purple bookmark sticking out of it. He fails to hide his grin though.

On Friday she comes into his room to tell him it's time for bed half an hour after it was time for bed and he sees the red mark on her nose where she has been pushing up her reading glasses. She presses a kiss to his forehead and tells him he's growing up so fast.

She goes through all her usual warnings and instructions as she drives him to Mike's sleepover but somewhere in between them her thoughts seem to drift off and she asks if they have any cookies left. As if they ever run out.

Mike's dad drops him off on Sunday. He watches his mom flush when she opens the door in her pyjamas. She guides him into the kitchen, asking if he's had any breakfast as she makes her coffee in the extra large „tough case" mug, yawning and rubbing her eyes. She doesn't even have a case.

When he sits down to breakfast on Thursday, she pushes a plate of pancakes toward him, leans her elbows on the table, winks at him conspiratorially and asks if he thinks Mrs. Pike will mind terribly, if he skips the last class next Wednesday so they can get in line at Castle Books earlier.

He fistpumps the air and drags her into a hug that puts her hair in the blueberry jam but she doesn't seem to mind one bit.

David grins at the little boy before him and leans as far as the big wooden desk will allow him.

"And what's your name?"

The kid smiles so wide David thinks his dimples will never let up after this.

"Damon!"

"And do you have a favourite character, Damon?" he asks with a smile, trying to maintain eye contact with the boy, while he twists his usual inscription a bit to make it more personal.

"Uh-ha. The King of the Lake!"

"The King of the Lake. A noble ruler, if I've ever written one. Good choice, though he is a bit of troublemaker. Don't worry, I won't tell Santa," he whispers and winks at the man standing behind the boy.

"Just like daddy!"

David gives "daddy" an inquisitive, amused look.

"Oh, not the troublemaker part. I work at the lake so…," the man explains with a chuckle, looking a bit flustered at having the spotlight on him.

David laughs and motions for the other book they've brought. Tina – usually quick to scold him for asking more than one question and signing more than one book per fan, is uncharacteristically, suspiciously quiet on his left and he intends to take full advantage of it.

Glancing at his manager, he doesn't find her distracted and tapping away on her phone as he expected but apparently enchanted by the twin set of dimples before him.

David's faith in magic and happy endings is far from what it used to be when he first moved to the States but one can't exactly write fairytales for a living, albeit unorthodox ones, and not preserve some spark of hope and belief in his heart. It just comes with the territory. So with a devious smirk at his manager and a hastily half-formed plan, he turns to Damon's father with a serious, 99% professional expression. A percent of the deviousness he finds himself unable to purge. He gives the man's hands a quick scan and proceeds.

"Speaking of professional matters, they are currently casting the characters for the first movie. I believe we are having some trouble finding a good fit for a certain little duke."

Tina makes some sort of a choked sound behind him. It is the least graceful thing he has ever heard from her and it only further cracks his professional façade. Deviousness at 10% now.

"I know child acting is not to all parents' taste but perhaps my manager can give you her number and we can send you the audition details, if you're interested."

He watches the man's eyes widen in surprise and then shift to Tina and then… well, David might be a bit rusty in the romantic department but he is pretty sure that in books like his own stares like that are referred to as "one for the ages". So he turns his attention back to little Damon, who has been rummaging through his backpack, oblivious to his scheming, and is now showing him a drawing of what appears to be a man with a crown riding a very happy dolphin.

"Why, that's quite impressive. Would you like me to sign it?"

The boy shakes his head, his blond locks flying everywhere and his dimples flashing again and David doesn't know about Tina but he sure has been won over twice by now.

"For you."

"It's for me?"

The eager nod and the thought of having something to hang on his fridge thugs on his heart and he finds himself clearing his throat before speaking again.

"Then I believe you should sign it for me."

The boy looks beyond thrilled to take over as the star and David hands him his golden pen all too eagerly, instructing him to keep his wild scribble of a signature to the right corner of his drawing.

"Ah, thank you," he grins and takes back the pen when it

looks like Damon will be quite willing to sign the desk as well. "I think your dad will be happy to take you for a hot chocolate or something equally delicious now."

He turns to look at the father in question who has moved closer to his manager so they can awkwardly exchange numbers under the pretext of formal arrangements that sound more fictitious than anything he's ever written.

"Oh, yes, of course! Come on, Damon."

David watches the boy bounce over the few feet to his father and grin up at Tina with all the cuteness that melted his own heart. She proves just as helpless to his charms as she crouches down in her five-inch heels to shake his little hand.

With a chuckle he turns to thank the patient person that waited for that whole fiasco to play itself out without a word or throat clearing of complaint.

"That was awesome!"

The boy, about twice Damon's age, beams up at him as if he just moved a mountain and not simply sign a couple of books and play questionably successful matchmaker. But David is delighted to encounter another enthusiastic child so he smiles right back, wide and genuine. Then his eye catches the hand on the boy's shoulder and moves up a wool-clad arm to take in one of the loveliest women he has had the good fortune of meeting today.

He feels his jaw go a little slack — no doubt turning his smile a shade idiotic, but finds himself unable to do much about it when confronted with the brown-haired ball of energy and the guardian angel behind him, who seems to be doing her damnest to suppress a grin and failing spectacularly. The amused twinkle in her eyes and the becoming colour high on her plump cheeks don't help either.

"That was quite the matchmaking," she teases and he swears his heart stutters for the first time in almost a decade.

On the 20th it takes Alyson over an hour to put her kid to bed. She gives two solid tries to convincing him that Mr. Arkwright won't be able to sign more than one book (maybe two, if Alyson *pretends* to be a fan herself) and then repeatedly assures him that she put all three of his favourite editions in a tote bag by the door, and then finally lets him out of bed so he can see for himself.

She spends a good fifteen minutes reassuring him that David won't cancel the event and silently swears to every god she doesn't believe in that she will hunt the man down and drag him in front of her son with a Santa hat and bells on top, if he doesn't show up.

But her research says that he has yet to bail on any commitment in the last three years and the thought of him in a Santa hat and nothing else jumps unbidden in her mind and has nothing to do with dragging him into her apartment for the benefit of her son.

The day itself Ben spends on cloud nine. She has trouble convincing him to at least have some eggs for breakfast and then she has even more trouble convincing him that queuing at the bookstore from the moment it opens isn't more important than going to school.

When she comes to pick him up, he is waiting for her at the gate and she has barely killed the engine when he runs around the car with a grin the size of which she worries might do permanent damage to his face.

Once inside the bookstore, he is almost trembling with not-at-all-suppressed excitement and she has to warn him to cool the jets or she'll have to take him to the doctor instead of David Arkwright. He looks so horrified at the mere suggestion that she raises her hands in willing surrender.

The atmosphere in the store helps a bit. She has to give it to this guy, he has won over everyone from two-year-olds who, by the looks of their cosplaying parents, are being raised with his books, to the elder manager of the bookstore herself, who has allowed hot drinks and sweets to be sold on the first floor for the first time.

Alyson gets a cup of hot chocolate with tons of whipped cream and a bag of marshmallows for Ben. With the way the boy's hands are shaking, he'll spill any liquid all over his favourite editions and then— she is too afraid to let her imagination go down that road.

When they draw near the centre of the second floor, where a neat circle has been cleared out and a desk set up for Mr. Arkwright, she begins to catch glimpses of black hair and a dark blue shirtsleeve. And if she goes on her tiptoes a bit to do so — well, that's her own damn business and anyway she saw a blond with a t-shirt that read "David Arkwright owns this prince's heart (and everything else)" so whatever, they all know what they are here for.

They are five people away when she gets a good look at him – much less threatening in real life though she can tell even from behind the desk that he will tower over all the children gathered around in a way very reminiscent of a certain giant scene in book IV (man, she knows what's in which book now). But the careful, deliberate way he signs the books in his hands and the way he tilts his head to the side, as if he's really listening to everyone that comes before him – she can't imagine this guy squashing a bug, let alone scaring children. And if the enthusiasm of the ones waiting to meet him is any indication, they can all sense that.

He tenses a bit when an overly enthusiastic couple lean in on either side of him and wrap their arms around his neck to take a selfie. Alyson watches him drop his hands in his lap and sketch a polite smile as his manager steps in to ask the overzealous fans to hurry up.

She makes a note to keep an eye on the efficient brunette in the killer heels because Ben will certainly be one of those people that need prompting to leave the author's side.

The little boy in front of them seems almost as excited as Ben and her son, wonderful kid that he is, patiently listens to him babble about his favourite character and answers all his questions about one of the multiple kingdoms in the books.

Then Damon steps forward and hefts his book on Mr. Arkwright's desk and Alyson watches the action unfurl before her.

She has no small amount of trouble reconciling what she knows about this guy with the patiently engaging and sweetly mischievous man a few feet from her. She can almost feel the grudging respect for his talent and rise from the ashes stretch and transform itself into passionate admiration for the unyieldingly kind and wonderful human he appears to be.

He hasn't even said a word to them yet and she is already beyond grateful that her son gets to meet this man.

Ben can barely restrain himself as he watches Damon get to talk to David and he facepalms internally for not thinking to bring him one of his own drawings as well. Then he quickly reassures himself that he is too grown up for that.

When he sees the boy move over and shake hands with the woman that seems to work with David, he can't contain himself any longer.

"That was awesome!"

David looks at him and smiles widely. Then he looks at his mom and his face reminds Ben of that time Miss Blair took them to the archaeological museum and the guy at the entrance couldn't stop staring at her and managed to mix up their tickets three times. He finds it interesting how two completely different faces can wear almost identical expressions.

"That was quite the matchmaking."

"I try. Happiness found in the most unlikely of places and all that."

David purses his lips as if he is about to say something more, but then just shakes his head and looks back at him, his smile returning to its welcoming and put-together shape.

"So what's your name then?"

"I…"

Oh. *Oh.*

Ben tries swallowing a couple of times and opens his mouth again but nothing comes out.

Oh.

David Arkwright is waiting to hear his name and he can't make words come out of his mouth.

"Ben?"

His mom's voice comes from behind him, confused and a little concerned. He is about to try saying something to her at least when David gets up and comes to sit on the ground, leaning his back against the desk he was just sitting at, so that Ben has to look down at him now.

"No worries, my boy. I'm not partial to old warlock tricks, won't use your name for anything nefarious," he grins and extends his hand. "I'm David."

No kidding, he wants to say but feels himself smiling instead. He swallows one more time and finally manages to convince his vocal cords to work.

"I'm Ben."

His arm moves as if on its own and Ben sighs in relief when he manages to shake hands like a normal person.

"Pleasure to make your acquaintance, Ben," David says with a satisfied grin. "I take it you like my books?"

He hears his mom snort above them but pays her no mind. He is talking to David Arkwright.

"Yeah. They… they are pretty great."

That was lame but David's grin grows and— David Arkwright shook his hand.

"Do you have a favourite?"

He is talking to David Arkwright.

She can say she's not charmed by his matchmaking ways but why lie to herself?

She can say his eyes are not the most calming green.

She can say her heart doesn't tremble when Ben's voice catches on his own name and he stares at his idol like a baby deer caught in fucking floodlights.

She can say that same heart doesn't do three consecutive summersaults when David sits down at her son's feet and coaxes his name out with the care and patience.

She can say she doesn't practically glow with happiness and pride when Ben suddenly rushes into a lengthy explanation of why the first, fourth and fifth books are his favourite.

She can say David doesn't glow almost as brightly when her son explains how much he wants to become a writer just like him and how excited he is for the first movie even though it can't possibly be as good as the book.

She can say it all makes her picture Ben with a father figure in his life – just a general father figure, not this precise man, who is looking at her kid as if every word out of his mouth is the gospel truth.

But why lie to herself?

David ignores the first throat clearing and curses silently. He thought Damon's dimples will buy him more time. Then again, he has been conversing with Ben for a rather long time – genuinely taken with the boy's unrestrained enthusiasm, even if he keeps sneaking glances at his beautiful mother, smiling tentatively at the two of them.

The second throat clearing catches said mother's attention and he watches her glance apologetically, yet somewhat defiantly, at his manager. He backs her up with a completely unapologetic scowl at Tina.

"Well, Ben, did you bring any of those favourites for me to sign?"

"Oh, right. Sorry!"

It's Ben's mom that replies as she bends to pull the heavy books (his favourite editions) from her tote bag, her hair falling in front of her like a curtain.

"Which one, kid?" she says firmly, giving her boy a look that seems to be both warning and beseeching.

He is all too willing to come to her aid.

"Nonsense. You lugged those things here, the least I can do is sign all of them."

He catches a glimpse of Ben's triumphant look and gives him a glare for sassing his mother as she drops down to her knee, joining him on the soft green carpet and leaving the boy towering over the both of them.

"Sorry to take so much of your time," she says following another louder throat clearing from Tina.

"You can make amends to my manager but personally, I'm having the time of my life."

She quirks a disbelieving eyebrow at that and he gives her his most winning and sincere smile. Then he grabs the first book and takes his sweet time writing an inscription for Ben, encouraging him in his writing pursuits. He's signing his name when he feels a pang at the thought of not seeing those pursuits play out. He furrows his eyebrows and thinks he can ask for their last name and goggle the boy in a few years. It doesn't quite satisfy him but it will have to do.

He draws a quill pen on the next book before signing it but then hesitates when he puts the third one on his knee. He bites his lip and glances up at the almost-black eyes staring back at him.

"Perhaps I can make this one out to you, Mrs...."

He feels a hopeless, unreasonable but thrilling, little spark shoot through him as he waits for her answer.

She swears they have been sitting there, monopolizing David's time for a solid 5 minutes now but every time she even thinks about urging Ben to go, some part of her slaps her upside the head and tells her to let her kid enjoy the numbered moments he gets to spend in his presence. His very endearing, completely disarming presence.

So she listens to herself and watches the way his lashes lower as he bends his head to draw an intricate (absolutely adorable, who-the-hell-does-that, what-even-is-this-man) little quill on Ben's book. She listens to her son's excited intake and feels herself sigh and dig her knee deeper into the carpet beneath her. She looks at the strands of hair falling over his forehead and balls her hand into a fist so she doesn't reach out and push them back.

And then she is looking into his eyes and—

"Perhaps I can make this one out to you, Mrs.…."

She doesn't consider the possibility that he is inquiring after anything other than her name like she usually would. She is too busy pretending she wasn't blatantly staring at him. Yet some blessed part of her (probably the slap-happy part) has the good sense to correct him anyway.

"Rose. Miss Rose. Alyson Rose."

She blushes and concentrates all her efforts on not swearing out loud.

"Rose."

He seems to consider it. Then he bends over the book again. Once he is done, she expects him to get up and resume his seat but he reaches for the second book again and adds something to the inscription, then he hands it back to Ben and finally gets to his feet. Alyson is about to do the same when he offers her his hand.

She takes it and tells herself not to use any bodice-ripper clichés. Even just in her head. It's quite difficult. Especially when he brushes his lips over her knuckles after tugging her to her feet.

"It was an absolute pleasure to meet you, Ben," he says with a megawatt smile when he turns to her son and bends down a little to look him in the eyes and stage-whisper. "I look forward to coming to you for an autograph one day."

He winks at the boy, straightens and gives her one last long look that she can't quite read but which bears inexplicable amounts of apprehension and anticipation.

When they finally move away, books hugged to both their chests, his manager looks beyond relieved to see them go.

They are almost out the door when Alyson comes to a halt. Ben gives an excited cheer behind her.

"Mom! Look! He drew a rose beside the quill."

She doesn't respond. She is too busy staring at the phone number in the book in her hands.

3.
The Legend of Decaris

"Ever heard the legend of Decaris?"

"That's not a thing."

"No?"

"No, pretty sure you just made that up and – if we consider how the human brain works – we can probably even determine what objects and events from the last day made you pick the name Decaris."

"Wow. Seriously? We're literally lying under the Northern Lights on Christmas Eve, sharing a blanket and some heavily spiked cocoa and you are giving me a lesson in neuroscience."

"Hardly. Psychological association at best and on a very basic level at that."

"Mikey, just... shut up. You're sucking the magic out of this. Also – you're wrong."

"Am I?"

"Indeed. What is a legend?"

"Dunno. A story passed down from generation to generation?"

"Precisely. And you, you lucky bastard, are about to witness the birth of a legend. If you can just shut your mouth long enough."

Mike mimics zipping his lips and watches him sigh in exasperation and reach over to mimic locking them with a key instead and then throwing it away.

"It's more poetic. I'm about to tell you a grand tale, don't "zip" stuff."

He grins – careful not to open his mouth – and settles into his role of "stuff", laying his head on his boyfriend's shoulder and waving his hand towards the glorious sky above them, motioning for him to proceed.

"Right, let's see. Once upon a time— no, much before that actually, when the oceans lay flat and motionless, the wind rushed to and fro above them – lonely but very busy. It loved telling you that – how busy it was, if you managed to catch it for a spell. The wind was never light or playful back then – it had too much to do, no time to chat or enjoy itself, no time to take a pretty leaf for a spin just because. The oceans hardly did a thing – the wind had to fill the ships' sails, push them forward and hold them back all on its own. Every gust had to be weighed and measured, perfectly calculated and executed.

Decaris was the son of a powerful man – the man who created the waves. Each and every single one. Because, you see, all the waves that will ever be have already been created. They have been rising and crashing from the moment his father called them forth and released them upon the oceans and will be rising and crashing until there are oceans to carry them. But the waves were not like the wind. They delighted in their tasks awhile and then quickly grew truant and wild, chasing each other around, trying to see which could rise the highest, foam the whitest, and completely forgetting their duties.

So Decaris was tasked with guiding the waves whenever they strayed and he did so with will beyond that of any man, god or force of nature. Before long, the waves were lapping at his feet like faithful dogs, carrying him on their backs, twisting and turning, growing and shrinking at his command. He was impartial, he was just, he was unswayable. Or so his father believed and swore. Mind, the oceans believed the same and so did Decaris. Until he met a particular sailor.

Decaris liked to wash up on shore with his waves from time to time. Normally humans provided little amusement and could not hold his attention for long. Then came the port of Martha and a sailor that was about to change the seas and the skies forever without even knowing it.

Decaris had talked to humans before but never touched one. He was pleased to find that he could do so without either of them dissolving into drops of salt water.

A week later the sailor went back to his ship and Decaris went back to his waves. But while all the change in the former consisted of a propensity for wistful sighs and secretive smiles, the latter was altered on levels deeper than the very oceans he ruled.

Decaris had grown partial. He steered waves away from his sailor's ship or drove them under its massive body to help it outrun its enemies. The ones that tried to bury the ship he stole from the oceans. Some say he put them in his pockets – the waves, that is – which is nonsense, of course. He had no use for pockets in the water, all the cover he needed was made of sea foam. But he must have put them somewhere to contain their tumultuous nature and prevent them from fulfilling their duty.

You see, his sailor's ship was meant to sink and wave after giant wave was sent to wreck it and plunge it into the inky depths below. Even Decaris could not protect it from every wave, no matter how many he captured. Eventually the ship met its delayed fate and with it went Decaris' sailor.

But his secret did not have the luck of sinking to the bottom of the ocean with him. His father had got wind of his son's betrayal of the waves long ago and had given him as many chances to repent as he possibly could. No matter who he was by blood and how great his talents, Decaris had violated his father's trust and worse yet – the trust of the waves. He had defied the order of the oceans. So the night after the sailor's demise – black as the heart of a sea serpent – the father banished his son to the northernmost point of the world, where no wave was ever to reach his feet again."

The wind whispers around them, as if it is loath to disturb the beauty above and the peace below. People are rarely as considerate as the wind.

"Oh, come on, don't do that."

"Do what?"

"Pause for dramatic effect."

"I am not, we are just about to move on to the next part of the story – I'm giving you time to assimilate."

"All assimilated here, go on."

"Impatience. I can work with that. Alright.

You'd think Decaris was all alone in his exile. And he thought so too. He'd resolved himself to eternal mourning and loneliness. He was, of course, immortal and it was quite the task to move on from someone when you have been banished to the edge of the world with no one around and nothing but memories and dreams to keep you company.

But one night, lying on the cold ground as we are – mind, he did not have such a cushy pillow as you – he realized how many stars there were above him. At first, he watched them in awe, in reverence, in trepidation. Some nights he tried to count them though he knew very well that it was a useless and endless endeavour. Perhaps that is why he was doing it. He recited all the constellations he had been taught and after a while started making his own. At times it seemed to him that the stars were humouring him – shifting and rearranging themselves to suit his fancy. Eventually, he started talking to them.

Some say they were touched by his story and adopted him as their own. Some say he fell in love with a star and was shown their secret ways. Some say the stars were so taken with his tales that they wished to keep him forever to entertain them in their own solitude. That's no trifle.

You can easily convince the waves to play with you, though you should never venture too far into the sea when you do, tempt the wind to race you, though you should run with the full confidence of a loser, and the sands are notoriously weak-willed and easy to mould to suit your preference and pleasure. But not the stars. The stars are beyond all that. To talk to the stars is one thing, to have them listen – one must realize they are bombarded with silly wishes at all times – is a true honour, and to have them respond – almost unheard of.

What they told him is unknown. But what the story tells us is how one day the loneliness and distance became too much for Decaris. So he climbed to the highest spot on the northernmost point of the world, where he had not seen or felt a wave in ages and had dreamt of little but his lost sailor, and he begged the stars to take him with them. They say there was no moon that night and the stars felt bold and mischievous. They were much too attached to Decaris now to leave him in his despair. So they brought him to the sky.

What they did not know and Decaris had long forgotten were all the waves he had stolen, all the waves in his none-pockets. Up they went with their master and keeper and, as he raced towards his beloved stars, they spilled out over the sky – wave after wave, each brilliant and unique. Decaris looked back and felt salt roll down his cheeks at the beautiful sight, but he dared not turn and forsake his salvation. All he could do was watch as the waves spilled over the North – each its own colour – marking his path through the sky."

He looked down at the man leaning on his shoulder, his nose digging lightly into his collarbone, the lights above playing over his light features and casting him in a rainbow of colours.

"That's a hell of a breadcrumb trail to leave."

"Well, you know, some men have a flair for the dramatic."

"You would know."

"Hush now or I won't tell you the one about the North Star and its mistress."

4.

Scotch-tape Me Back Together

This. Next time Alexandra asks why he doesn't want to go to her annual Christmas party, he will cite this precise moment in space and time – his hair falling in his eyes, sweat gathering at his neck, 4 out of his 5 fingers with scotch tape stuck on them (leaving him with nothing but futile puffs of air to remove the aforementioned hair from his line of sight), holding down one end of the wrapping paper with his knee, a mostly empty cup of not-so-hot-anymore tea leaving a ring on another, and the remaining two ends curling in on him like tidal waves intent on choking the last breath out of him and plunging him firmly into chaos and despair.

Is he being overdramatic? Perhaps. Is he at the end of his tether? Almost. Does he regret ever agreeing to take part in Alex's Secret Santa? Abso-fucking-lutely. Or, to be more precise, it is her "seasonal wrapping mandatory" clause that has prompted the invention of some brand new curse words over the last hour and a half.

He has one hand, for fuck's sake. He thinks he should be allowed a damn "terribly impersonal" gift bag. Admittedly, he never asked her to make an exception, seeing as he doesn't want to be the fucking exception, he doesn't want extra attention, he most definitely doesn't want *special treatment*.

So here he is – scotch-taped to a red sheet of paper with golden stars and Christmas trees on it. Maybe next time he'll take someone up on the fucking special treatment.

Sometimes he thinks wistfully back to his life a mere two years ago, before he befriended Marco Ricci and subsequently his wife and subsequently every living creature (human and mammal alike) in the village of Positano. Maybe he was smoking and drinking and eating a bit too much, spending more time with his characters than actual people, but at least he didn't have glittering bows stuck to the edge of his sleeve.

But it is too late for that now. It was probably too late the moment the robust Italian clapped him on the back and appointed himself as his guide in the vast territories of Positano (all 8.65 square kilometres of them). A week later his tourist status was irrevocably lost. A month later he had met a thousand people more than he originally intended to when moving to the coastal village – half-determined to live on his boat and have only the amount of human contact required to not live solely on fish for the rest of his life. At least on that account he has been unquestionably successful. No person who knows Alexandra Ricci can ever fall prey to a poor diet.

Now he is beginning to see what the true price of friendship and nutrition is.

Sighing in defeat, he lifts his knee and watches the paper roll in on itself and surround his cup. If cups could glare…

He goes to the kitchen island and methodically sticks every tiny piece of scotch tape on the edge so he can convince them to release his fingers. He has no desire to lose the other hand as well. And to freaking stationery no less.

He glances back at the sad mess in the middle of his living room. A gorgeous set of wine glasses and the wrapping catastrophe around them.

His main problem – the way he sees it (aside from the obvious), is that every person he is on good enough terms with to ask for help is going to the damn party. And since the Riccis' brilliant Secret Santa is designed so that everyone leaves their present under the ostentatiously large tree and then randomly picks one, he has no idea who will receive his present. And if Alex learns that he revealed his gift to anyone beforehand… Better brave the stationery.

Which leaves him with only one other option. A neighbour.

Now, he likes to think that he has been nothing but courteous to all his neighbours. Recently. However, he had been living in this building for a few months before he met Marco and gradually decided to not be the crazy hermit guy. Those weren't exactly good months. Hence, why his neighbours may be acquainted with his less than courteous side. And why, generally, excluding the Riccis and their large, *large* circle of friends, he still likes to keep to himself as much as one can in a village the size of a saucer.

But desperate times call for desperate measures. And some

balls.

So, with another sigh of resignation and a mental pep talk – the gist of which is 'yes, you had a pathetic 'woe is me' phase and people witnessed it and those people still live and breathe at very close proximity but you'll just have to suck it up and do this so you don't disappoint the new people in your life who don't know any better than to be in it' – he considers his options.

He visualises the rusty mailboxes downstairs and starts going down the list of names. His face contorts in a seemingly endless series of frowns, cringes, nose-bridge pinches, forehead furrows, eye squeezes and some more cringes. And then – Ross.

His brow smooths out and he considers it. He knows very little, especially considering that he has access to Alexandra's vast – he is inclined to say bottomless – knowledge of Positano and its denizens.

Elza Ross came back by ferry from Poseidon-knows-where less than a year ago to claim her late grandmother's small apartment. She had exactly one suitcase, two duffel bags and one laptop bag. Before she used to visit her grandmother on her birthday, never on Christmas. She goes to the same bakery every three days. She picks fruits from trees that have found themselves outside of the purview of private gardens. She is a translator of sorts. In the late afternoons, more often than not, she can be found in whatever corner of the beach is seeing the least activity that day. It is all circumstantial and filtered through the gossip mill because she has kept to herself in a much more successful fashion than he has.

But none of that really matters. No, what matters is that she missed his self-dubbed pathetic 'woe is me' phase. He has been nothing but an exemplary neighbour – helping her with her luggage – despite her initial reluctance, when she moved into the building, bringing her a cup of coffee – despite her initial reluctance, when she locked herself out of her new dwelling a couple of weeks ago. He may stumble over the polite/awkward line sometimes but, unless his imagination is playing tricks on him, which – entirely possible, she seems to find that more amusing than off-putting.

However, that plan has a couple of flaws.

#1 Just because she wasn't around to witness his Worst Hits, doesn't mean she hasn't heard all about them. No, not with Mrs. Chiellini living across from her. He is labouring under no such delusions.

#2 Just because Miss Ross might be willing to help him, it doesn't automatically mean he is willing to ask.

If he needed help installing something on his computer, that would be a different thing. But he is no idiot and he isn't much for vacations by The Nile. He has a thing about asking for help with things he would've been perfectly capable of handling by himself, if he – you know, had the full set of appendages advisable. He thinks most people in his position have such a thing. His therapist tells him so as well.

So the real question is exactly how much scotch he needs to swallow his pride with.

The answer is none.

If he is going to make himself into a charity case, he thinks he can at least be a sober charity case.

Miss Ross answers her door on the second knock, which is fortunate since he isn't sure how soon he would've shrugged, told himself 'well, you gave it a solid try, man' and ran off.

She looks surprised to see him but not strictly unpleasantly so. He takes that as a decent start. Then he takes in her black leggings and her baggy Iron Man t-shirt and the hair spilling from her bun and the spot of what seems a lot like peanut butter on her cheek and he even manages to crack a smile.

Elza inclines her head to the side and frowns when he points to the place where some of her breakfast (afternoon snack? who has peanut butter at 4 pm?) remains. She seems to get the hint after a couple of tries and swipes hurriedly at the cheek that is taking on a slightly rosier hue.

He allows himself to grin at her as she clears her throat and straightens her shoulders as if to erase that little moment from her memory. He knows a thing or two about selective memory for the sake of preserving one's sanity and dignity.

"Can I help you?" she finally asks, her voice not unkind but not terribly welcoming either.

But then again "welcoming" has never been the first word to pop into his head when he sees Elza Ross. Intriguing, haggard, fierce, on occasion intimidating, on occasion enticing, once completely frazzled, never really welcoming.

He is alright with that. He isn't one to talk.

"Hi."

He immediately regrets not rehearsing this conversation. It's an exhausting habit that he has been trying to kick – going over every potential social interaction in his head before he is forced to actually go through it in real life. He's getting pretty good at just "rolling with it" as Alex puts it, so, naturally, here is the one time he wishes he had prepared beforehand.

"I… was indeed hoping that you might be able to assist me."

She rolls her eyes and he is pretty sure it has to do with the way he turned her words around to make them three times their length.

"And what do you need „assistance" with?"

"Gift-wrapping."

Her eyebrows jump to her hairline and she snorts. He is well on his way to taking offense and tucking his tail between his legs to beat a hasty retreat when she decides to elaborate on the derisive sound.

"You couldn't have picked a worse door to knock on. I'm like, a disaster in anything aesthetic. Or whatever."

She waves her hand around to encompass "whatever" and scrunches up her nose adorably and it does wonders for his nerves.

"Well, at least you have two of these," he says lightly, pointing to the hand still making vague gestures in front of her.

Her expression shifts but he feels another small doze of nerves seep out of him when she doesn't go for sympathy or distress or discomfort or any in the gallery of emotions that he has come to expect. She seems almost surprised. And while he is absolutely certain she couldn't have missed that particular detail, she genuinely looks like she forgot all about it.

It makes the tense grin on his lips relax into a more natural one.

"Alright then," she says with a shrug. "But don't say I didn't warn you."

"You could've just brought the thing to my place, you know?"

"You are already doing me a favour, I'm not going to inflict the wrapping paper nightmare on your apartment."

"Yeah, let's wait for the end result before we label this a "favour", I—"

That's when she steps into his living room.

"Whoa."

"Yeah," he chuckles nervously and squints at the sight before them. "Can't say I didn't give it a try."

He definitely tried.

All his furniture is pushed to the periphery of the room so there's nothing at the centre but all manner of stationery – scissors, glue, freaking paper clips (he doesn't know, alright? he was desperate!), the accursed scotch tape and, of course, three different rolls of wrapping paper and about a dozen bows and ribbons. Every nearby surface – from his small coffee table to the kitchen island – is covered in bits of scotch tape.

There are numerous cups with different liquids, none of them actually on the coffee table, representing the five stages of gift-wrapping: tea – obvious denial of what's to come, scotch – anger at his complete inability to cope with the simple task, coffee – bargaining, perhaps he simply wasn't awake enough yet and it could all work out with an extra dose of caffeine, soda – depression and a desperate need for a sugar rush, back to tea – acceptance of his failure.

Elza ventures into the holiday-sponsored disaster sooner than he expects and goes around sniffing all of the cups and glasses before picking up the one with some dregs of coffee at the bottom.

"I'll have some of that."

Her hair is falling in her eyes, sweat is gathering above her lip, 7 out of her 10 fingers have scotch tape on them (leaving her with no option but to keep asking him to push the hair away from her face), she is holding one end of the wrapping paper down with her elbow, a mostly empty cup of not-so-hot-anymore coffee leaving a ring on another, and the remaining two ends curling in on her much like she is curling her tape-littered fingers around his heart with every passing second.

"Get this one off my finger!" she waves her left hand in his face and he liberates her thumb.

"Why did you put one on your thumb? That's the only one I always leave free."

"Oh, so *now* you're a wrapping expert?"

"I would've been done with this ages ago, if I had your number of fingers."

"Yes, well, some of us are just as hopeless at this with all hands on board. I did warn you."

He lifts both arms in a clear show of surrender. Honestly, he has no right to bitch about the fact that this is taking her forever since he is shamelessly enjoying watching her huff and curse at the paper and tape in and all over her hands.

"Alright! This… this looks decent, right?"

It looks horrendous but her face is so anxious yet hopeful and the way she is biting her lip makes her look years younger, and he doesn't have the heart to point out the edge where you can see the box peeking out.

"Far superior to anything I could've accomplished."

She gives him a look that tells him she is half-offended by the not-exactly compliment and half-grateful that he didn't straight out lie to her.

"OK, pick a ribbon!"

He grabs one of the less flashy golden ribbons and hands it to her with great ceremony. Elza huffs and bends over the present once again and he goes back to watching in fascination the way she cranes her neck this way and that, the way her cheeks flush a little when the ribbon slips from her fingers, the way the tip of her tongue peaks from the edge of her mouth when she thinks she's got it.

"Put a finger here."

He shakes his head and hurries to comply.

"No, over it. I think."

"Like this?"

"Yes. Now— Ugh!" her growl is an animalistic thing at this point – 99% pure malice and 1% tortured whine. "Just— get it out of my face or I'll take those scissors and I don't know if my hair or your present will be the first to go."

He has the nerve to chuckle under his breath and moves to retrieve his hand from the ribbon tying procedure.

"NO! Don't you dare!"

"The hair or the ribbon?"

"Do you need your hand to move my hair?"

He swears he feels his heart stutter in his chest at that. Fuck. He tries to remember if he has touched anyone with the stump of his left arm before. It's a stupid attempt to regulate his breathing. He knows he hasn't.

And he's not— He doesn't want to— That is, he has nothing against it but she—

"Well?"

99% tortured whine and 1% malice now.

He swallows and feels incredibly aware of every inch of his being as he shuffles forward on his knees and lifts his left arm to move the pivotal strand of hair that's right in front of her eye. His sleeve slides down a little and his scarred flesh barely brushes her cheek before he drops his elbow back to his thigh and she sighs in utter relief.

"Thank you! Now—"

It takes them three tries to make the damn bow look somewhat decent.

Once at his door, Elza seems intriguingly reluctant to cross the threshold.

"So. Umm, I might call you up, if I need any wrapping of my own. Since we obviously need at least two heads and three hands between us to get the job done."

She shrugs – half-smiling, half-cringing, as if she is not sure she can make a joke like that. He grins at her, nodding his assent.

"Always at your service, Miss Ross. Thank you and sorry for taking so much of your time."

She waves him off, scrunching up her face in that way he is quickly becoming terribly enamoured with.

"Please, I'm pretty sure this tops scrolling Instagram while doing my laundry."

He nods again and watches her hesitate one more time. A small light seems to flicker through her eyes and she glances up. He frowns at her and then at the top of his door casing.

What is she looking fo—

Oh.

He never was one for Christmas clichés and now he is paying the price for it.

"Oh, well," Elza sighs, drawing his gaze back to hers. "I guess no excuse is still an excuse."

He feels a sharp tug on his Henley and then her lips are on his – warm and soft and tasting of his coffee and exploration and her peanut butter and impatience.

It is the best non-mistletoe kiss he has ever had. It is probably the best kiss he has ever had, period. Which doesn't stop him from letting out a gruff little laugh when they pull apart, her hands still on his shirt and his hand and stump resting lightly on her hips.

"No excuse is still an excuse?""

"Shut up."

"What's that even supposed to mean?"

"Do you want me to kiss you again or not?"

"Repeatedly."

They become notorious at the Riccis' Christmas parties. Or at least their presents do – the worst wrapped ones from the whole bunch.

They take special pride in it.

5.
The Fly

She misses the family with the two kids and the red, supernaturally loud coffeemaker. She knows a thing or two about the supernatural and she used to run her life on caffeine, PBJs and precious little else so it made her feel included, almost welcome in a way.

It's funny because she sure as purgatory hated them when they were around. The kids' stamping feet lost a fair bit of their preciousness when coupled with their wails and high-pitched screeches. (She is convinced they used to have a dog – they seem like the type that would have the two kids, the SUV and the dog – but then its eardrums could not withstand the pitches those children could reach when denied a second scoop of ice-cream and it ran away.)

The parents used to fight over the most mundane things. Admittedly, she has gained the kind of perspective few people have and with it a more solid idea of what is truly worth screaming or stewing over. But, regardless of that or maybe exactly because of it, they were truly depressing to watch.

Middle-aged, healthy, both in pretty good shape, neither cheating as far as she could see (and she could see basically everything), they seemed to lack any serious financial problems and their children, while noisy bastards, were not juvenile delinquents by any stretch of the imagination. Yet they still managed to find shit to argue about. Enough of it to bring the house down.

Not literally, of course. As if she'd let them disturb her eternal dwelling. No, they just brought their own home down, along with their marriage and probably some of their offspring's emotional availability. It's fine by her, really.

She just grew used to those two sets of feet constantly going in circles around the kitchen table. And the coffeemaker. Damn that infernal thing. She misses it.

People think empty haunted houses are disconcerting to say the least. They should try haunting empty houses. It's the spookiest shit ever. You'd think the house seemed peaceful, maybe a bit cold, maybe a bit depressing. But that's not it at all.

The cobwebs grow corporeal and visible after the first month. Dust becomes its own entity and dust bunnies are more like genetically modified rabbit monsters. There's always that one kitchen cabinet that was left slightly ajar or even completely, carelessly wide open and she watches as the days weigh on the door hinges. It's not something you notice, if you look at it every day or even every week, but after six weeks you can see it sagging just a little bit, just enough, so that you know when somebody does come around to close it eventually, it won't fit properly and they'll have to tug it up a bit to fit it into place.

If everything was properly cleaned out, there shouldn't be too many pests. But just like the spiders, the flies always find their way in and then – like the morons they are – can't find their way out. So they die, of course. And if they die on the ground or in one of the lamps or even on a windowsill, she can take it. But there's always one that decides to take its last breath (she is pretty sure flies breathe just kind of fuzzy on the details of how) right above the dining table or the kitchen counter and then that's its resting place. It falls on the thin layer of dust – the noise softened, barely audible. If a fly dies on a kitchen counter and there's no one to see it, is the fly really dead? 'Course, it is. She sees it – the annoying black spot, marring the pristineness of the off-white counter. But then again, she doesn't count.

And it only gets worse when the dust starts covering the fly as well. Where the hell does all the dust in the world come from? Did they explain that in Physics class? It sounds like something that should've been explained but she never did listen much to the Physics guy, who was mostly interested in what gravity did for his female students. If she could haunt the old bastard, he never would've got another good night of sleep. But that's not how it works.

So the fly stays. More fall. In thicker and thicker coffins of dust. And the cobwebs keep growing and the windows get spattered by the rain and even beneath the dust and dirt she can see the part of the carpet that's always in the sun around noon beginning to lose its vibrant purple colour.

And that's if everything was cleaned out all right and proper, but sometimes there's a window left ajar or a tap left dripping or a clock left ticking and those, naturally, drive her out of her damn mind. And the hinge keeps bending under the weight of the door – imperceptibly, gradually.

It's horrifying to witness. Even as someone who no longer carries human flesh meant for wrinkling and sagging and then rotting, she can still feel the disturbing chill, the shiver of premonition – watching how things just go on without us, how naturally, in comparison with our presence, our absence is eradicated.

Everyone thinks a house without people inside is empty. She wishes they were right every day. But a house without people is just that – a house without people. A sign of how little that matters, how little we matter.

They. She should say they. But it doesn't really make her feel any better.

The new guy won't last. She knows it by the count. 4 boxes, 2 suitcases and one pathetic-looking backpack. Not enough. Not enough of him for a house like this. The equipment that follows the day after is impressive but it's not him – it's not enough. Still, some music might be nice.

There is no music and he almost breaks the record.

Realistically, nothing can be worse than the one that drew pentagrams on the floor and almost had her spooked for a moment before he started calling for "Lucifer" (she's never wished to be seen more – her eyeroll was a thing of beauty). But as she watches this one struggle to open his third beer with his pepperoni-greased fingers, she can't help the shudder or the thought that he is the worst one yet.

He doesn't go out the first two weeks. The mere suggestion seems ludicrous, seeing as he barely moves inside as well. As far as she knows (and she knows most of everything that happens under this roof), he hasn't even set foot on the second floor. His boxes are still in the living room where he first deposited them one by one all by himself. One of them ended up over the stretch of carpet that was starting to fade and gives her the smallest amount of relief. His musical equipment is cluttered in the insufficient space of the hallway, making sure that if he isn't going out, no one else is coming in. He tells all the delivery guys to ring the back door.

The couch has become his fortress. It's not even a good couch. It's a less-than-pleasant, sickly green three-person that she was hoping the next one will replace. That obviously isn't happening. Most of the piece of furniture is lost under discarded, stained t-shirts and open notebooks. A pen is leaving a progressively growing, black ink strain on the left seat. He has already lost at least two socks from different pairs in the depths of the upholstery. He seems to be living out of the backpack on the floor. There are beer bottles, pizza boxes and bags of chips, creating a truly impressive, impenetrable perimeter around his couch island.

The coffee table in front of it has been shockingly spared – nothing but his black laptop resting on top of it. The kitchen remains unconquered as well. The fly is still there.

She is starting to believe that his enormous headphones have been surgically attached to his head. She can't remember seeing him without them. Sometimes he watches movies – old things that she saw when they were the latest hits, mostly he just listens to music. Occasionally he scribbles things in one of his numerous notebooks, mostly he just reads from them – lines that look smudged and old. Once or twice a week he writes an email. His inbox is always bursting and his phone is always on silent, its light blinking non-stop to inform him that he is missing the call of society. Yet no one other than delivery boys ever comes to the door – front or back. Maybe nobody knows which door they have to come to.

She glimpses enough to understand that he must be some big name in the music industry, some behind-the-curtains know-it-all. His mails are short and sound like someone giving out sentences. They're mostly death penalties, handed out flippantly by a judge who doesn't see human life as a very valuable commodity.

But she can't figure out the crux of it. Is this just how he exists? Is it some self-indulgent spell before he moves on with his real life? Was there a break-up? A tragedy? She's always been good at sniffing those out but he is giving her nothing.

Week 3 sees him gone for two whole days and then back to Couch Island, County Garbage. The plastic bags look like jellyfish washed up on shore. She has never seen a living one, she hates the idea that this guy has.

It's not that when you die things become pointless, it's just then that you realize how pointless certain things have always been. Being angry is chief among those. Utterly useless. She hasn't been truly angry in decades. Annoyed – constantly, angry – not once. All that tension gathering under your temple, festering in your lungs, bunching up your muscle tissue and making your veins zing in the worst possible way.

She used to have a short fuse, back when she was a proper part of the world. She thought she didn't have a fuse at all anymore, turns out it just grew very long and this fucker might be the first one to manage to burn it to the end.

She can take the garbage, she can take the grease and ink stains on the couch she doesn't like anyway, she can take his week-old stench, the unnatural quietness that was supposed to be over but is just amplified by the soundless bobbing of his mop of greying hair to a tune she is not privy to, she— she can't take the fly. But one fly is not going to break the camel's back. December might.

She doesn't need a tree or decorations, she doesn't need the smell of a used kitchen and any jingle tunes, she doesn't need a party or presents or any of that. But, she swears to the silver-grey void which she has discovered is the only thing that is eternal, if he spends Christmas on that couch in the company of beer cans and a two-day-old pizza, she will find out exactly what and how she can do to a living creature to scare the life out of them.

She still mostly has the house to herself, if you disregard the barely living form on the couch, which she often does for days on end.

The master bedroom has always been her favourite. Not because of the gigantic bed in the centre where she used to sneak under the covers and tickle her parents' feet, not because of the perfectly coordinated colour palette that she helped her mother pick out, not even because of the large windows that let in the morning sunshine just at the right moment. This was the room where her biggest and best present was always hidden, it's why she always left it for last then and why she always visits it first now.

There are so many pockets in the universe – designed and designated to fit all sorts of odds and ends, but her favourite have always been the Christmas ones. A place for all the real Christmas trees that are thrown away the day after New Year's. A place for all the wrapping paper and ribbons ruthlessly torn to pieces. A place for all the lost cards that never reached the right mailbox. A place – an abyss really, for all the ungiven Christmas gifts.

An idea rises unbidden but she quickly stuffs it back where it came from. There's an abyss for that as well – all the ideas that cross our minds, that are entertained only to never take form, to never materialize.

In the next blink she is downstairs. He is lying on his back and she blinks a few more times in rapid succession when she notices that the headphones are off. It's annoying to say the least. She doesn't need to provide moisture for her immaterial eyes, every time she blinks – she is just not there. Another one in a number of fascinating things you find out when you are dead – blinking out of existence is an actual thing.

But after every blink he is still there – headphoneless, on his back, staring blankly at the ceiling. Some of the cobwebs usurping the corners must catch and tangle in his peripheral vision but if they bother him, he does a masterful job of not showing it.

It's the 23rd, she is angry for the first time in decades, the idea has emerged, she has refused to materialize it, she has refused to condemn it to the abyss, as a result she has succeeded in just nurturing it further. The good ones are the hardest to throw away.

It's the 23rd, he is sitting on the floor, his back to the couch, staring at what her scavengered computer knowledge prompts her to call a music software, the headphones are back on. His eyes are bloodshot and she can't tell if the colours on his t-shirt are actually part of the design.

It's the 23rd, she cuts the cord on her own tug of war, reaches into the abyss with little knowledge and the kind of blind confidence that has worked for her on the few occasions when she tried to pull something like this in the past. She has never tried to pull something quite like this.

It's the 23rd, the little blue box sits on the corner of the coffee table, it has no bow or tag, it looks heavy for its size but weight is not exactly something she can measure anymore. She doesn't even know if it exists in the same world he does.

It does. A day and she can already see the little specks of dust that have settled on the velvety blue. She doesn't understand how he hasn't seen it, how he has explained it away if he has, how curiosity hasn't made him open it.

Curiosity is never pointless, no matter which stage of existence or non-existence you are in.

His laptop is shut, his phone is on his chest, forcefully warming the skin under which she is starting to doubt if his heart is beating at all. His ears must be vibrating enough to power his whole body, even she can hear some of the deafening music seeping out of their leather edges now. She was wrong about the pizza – he seems to be forgoing food today. He is still on his first beer.

She is angry, she is angry about being angry. Anger is pointless, jealousy – doubly so, frustration is just toothless anger, pity is a cheap knockoff of empathy, loneliness is pointless, worry is pointless, regret – the most nonsensical of them all.

She feels herself – what constitutes herself now – propelled forward by the vacuum of uselessness that she accumulated feeling all those things so many years ago. The pressure of it slams into the couch and she watches him crash to the floor in wide-eyed amazement. The headphones fly off and land with an impotent clatter. He rises quickly for a man who spends most of his time on the very brink of slipping into a coma. For a second, he looks straight at her and she swears she has done something terrible, stepped over some line that wasn't even meant to be drawn, disturbed a balance that was guaranteed and taken for granted, raptured universes, created paradoxes, annihilated laws beyond her comprehension. It's the longest second of her consciousness.

Then he looks away, looks around wildly and unseeingly, a bit indignant, a whole lot confused.

She feels herself deflate, the vacuum is gone. Maybe there is a use for even the most useless feelings after all, maybe they fill up the empty spaces that are left in our beings when all the useful parts have been fitted in. Maybe there are a lot of empty spaces.

She finds the box in the same corner of the coffee table — open and empty. She never finds out what was inside. It must have been something old and useless.

He owns ties and shirts. Several of them actually. He hangs them in the wardrobe with the creaking door — the one that you have to raise a bit to close it properly.

He must have thrown out the couch along with all the trash around it.

The fly is gone. She would cry with relief, if she could.

The noise of him is so much and so constant that it bears a twisted resemblance to the silence of before — both are deafening. She hasn't decided yet which kind of deaf she prefers to be.

There is no such thing as unfinished business. If you didn't finish it, it wasn't your business. Once you're done, you're done. You can't suddenly decide to go back and start messing around — fixing shit. All things she knows, learnt quickly and almost instinctively.

Yet here she is — definitely in business of some sort.

Sometimes — when he is tense enough to start throwing things other than his numerous stress balls — she can feel his negative energy in the air and she wishes she could tell him that stress is only useful for shortening one's lifespan.

Once he is gone for weeks and she thinks he isn't coming back. She can't decide how she feels about that and she uses the slick machines and heavy-duty headphones left lying around as an excuse not to.

Sometimes she doesn't come out for days, she hears the slamming of doors and the shower running, hears the microwave downstairs, music flowing out of speakers for a change, she hears the fly caught between the window and the screen door, the keys skittering over the polished wood of the hall table and leaving a little chip on the left corner, she hears the cap of his beer come off, the thud of a single set of footsteps on the stairs, the whine of the hinges of the sagging door.

Sometimes she tries to open a notebook – push it off the table, make it float in the air, lift the corner, see through the pages. She never succeeds.

Once he is humming something enticing and fun and she is following him around, nodding along, caught in the melody, she doesn't realize he is walking out the door until it's too late. She has never tried to do this. It's one of those things that she instinctively knew not to. The sun blinds her for the briefest of seconds, his hum – light and unbothered. Then everything goes grey.

She can still hear the hum for a while, then it stops as well – she can't even tell if it cut off abruptly or just faded away into the distance. She is left in silver darkness and silence – there's dust everywhere. Huh. Maybe this is where all the dust in the world comes from. She doesn't know how long she spends there – time is another human measure that she is not so good at measuring anymore. She would scream, if she could. If fear wasn't pointless. When the specks of dust rearrange themselves into mundane matter all around her, she finds herself back in the hallway. He is just walking in.

Sometimes she tries to touch him – just her fingertips against the strands of hair that stick out at odd angles when he falls asleep on his new and much more comfortable couch. Occasionally, she succeeds.

The following Christmas she pulls another ungiven gift from the abyss and leaves it on the coffee table beside the fly.

6.

Symmetry

He wakes up in the forest again. This is happening for the fifth year in a row. He is already getting tired of it.

As always, he doesn't remember what came before. Not precisely. Not that he tries very hard.

He remembers four walls and a skylight. Then darkness. Yet, even in the darkness, he could feel that he wasn't alone, the radiating presence of a multitude of bodies around him — each one in its own cocoon, he assumed, just like he was. It was the musty, boxed-in kind of darkness as well — almost cosy but not quite, too oppressive and claustrophobic for comfort. The in-ness of it still clings to him even though he has probably been outside for a few hours now.

The stars have come out. He has either forgotten what they look like or this angle makes them completely foreign to him, or — he feels like this is true even if it makes the least sense — the stars have altered completely. They shine alright. But their usually cold and detached silver glow seems more vivid now —

alive and colourful in a way that, depending which one he focuses on, the whole sky takes on a completely different hue.

The smell of pine is everywhere, the way it is every year. It's not his favourite but it sure beats the musk of bodies stuffed in an enclosed space, almost on top of each other. He takes a deep breath – the air is inexplicably warm and the openness and emptiness of the forest feels artificially achieved.

For a moment, he wonders if he has been a lab rat for the last five years. If so, he must be a very disappointing subject. It's ridiculous how bad the thought makes him feel. He looks up again – half-ready to beg the lab gods' forgiveness – but there's nothing but trees and colourful stars above. No moon. No gods. He can just make out the biggest and brightest star.

Is that what they call the North Star? He wishes he were a sailor. Maybe he is – in a life beyond this limbo, an immaterial existence made of sea spray, the smell of brine, the calls of sea gulls and a vast expanse of blue.

But the forest around him intrudes on the serene vision. It is slowly coming to life – flashes of golden movement to the north – whoever or whatever is there has not spotted him yet; an incessant buzz – the most annoying melody, patiently driving him mad; so many scents – mostly swallowed by the overpowering pine, but occasionally, reaching his nostrils via some mysterious aerial pathways. It all lends too much tangibility to this world he has found himself in. He longs for his blue mirage, for the solitude of it.

If he is a lab rat, he is probably not the only one.

He rolls over. It always takes his legs a while to remember how to work and he never quite knows how to help them. But the sooner he starts walking, the more time he will have before… before.

He focuses on the flickers of gold. They are in his way – the one he always takes – year in and year out. He doesn't remember but then he moves forward and steps into the knowledge, waiting there as if his past self left it behind for him to find.

He sees the golden hat before he sees the man under it. In his defence, the man is 50% hat. Then he sees the beard – it's so long that the wind sends it over his shoulder – scraggy, pitifully listless and pointless. He knows there is a plant that it reminds him of but, if he ever knew its name, it's long gone now. 50% hat, 30% beard, 20% man.

He looks around and frowns. The bearded guy is alone. He is never alone. Well, "never" is a pretty absolute term that he probably can't apply in his circumstances (if anyone can ever rightfully apply it), but he certainly wasn't alone the last four years. There was always another one – identical in a way that didn't force you to wonder or, even worse, ask if they were brothers.

He never knows how to start these conversations. He clears his throat.

The bearded man whirls around – startled and skittish in a way that goes above and beyond the little shock he gave him.

"Ah. Ah, it's you. You're still here. Good, good – that's good."

"Well, yes. Where is your—"

He waves his hand around like a half-idiot. They are *identical* and yet, it feels rude to just assume someone's relation to another, even when it is completely obvious.

"Oh. You don't know."

It's not a question. He doesn't answer non-questions. Frankly, he is a firm believer that you should aim to answer as few questions throughout your life as possible and you definitely shouldn't butt in with answers to non-questions.

"It was… just a few days before… you know, *before*. I didn't know that, of course. You know, you never know when you'll be back in. But I had a feeling, the ground was beginning to slope downwards, my beard was growing heavy."

He nods. He knows. He has his own ways of telling, they all do, he supposes.

"A-and I told him, told him, "Jimmy, hang in there, brother." I—"

In whatever life he had before this, he must have been terrible at comforting people. It's either the truth or a very good excuse because it keeps him rooted to the spot – just out of reach of the distraught man, trying to regulate his breathing or stifle his sobs, or maybe release his sobs – whatever he is doing definitely would've triggered a response from someone who wasn't absolutely terrible at comforting people.

"And I-I… well, I just watched him fall to pieces, you know? He just… he broke completely – nothing could be salvaged."

He goes to nod again – thinks better of it. There's no other way, really. You either keep it together and hang on or you break down and never come back. Well, no, he has heard stories of some who went over the deep end and then were brought back the following year – hell, even the same year. But those… it wasn't the same. They weren't like them. Him and the bearded men – man, and the one he is making his way to – they are the real deal. It's life or death for them – keeping their balance.

The thought makes him antsy. He wants to go, he should go. This all happened last year, what can he do? He can't turn back time, he isn't good at comforting. He is useless here. He can be useful somewhere else.

That's how people move on in his opinion. They realize their efforts are pointless, their grief – useless, their wishes – nonstarters. But most of all, they realize they can be useful somewhere else.

"I have to go."

He turns around and doesn't look back. Useful people can be quite rude.

He trudges on, he knows this road so well. Just on schedule, he starts getting too hot, the air is thick with scents now, adding their weight to the atmosphere he has to slice through – something nutty and something weirdly sweet sneaking in. He wretches, feels the stickiness at the back of his throat.

He wishes – not for the first time – that he could take off his coat, maybe his hat. He can't. He is less annoyed about that than he is about the fact that there is another moment – identical to this one, waiting for him in the future – when he will want to take off his coat again and he won't be able to *again* – there is a whole string of moments like this, stretching as far as his clairvoyant inner eye can see. Like those infinity mirrors at fairs, the ones facing each other and creating horrifying eternities – your reflection so far away from you and yet still so painfully the same – no change, no progress, just further away.

He is unsure if he has ever seen mirrors like those. Then again, how else would he know about them? How else would he know what a perfect metaphor they are for the limbo that is his existence now?

He takes comfort in his sure footsteps, in the crunch of needles, in the occasional snap of bark. This has always been easy. From the very first time he knew his way – up. It seemed utterly ridiculous to go any other way and equally ridiculous to stay in one place. That first night, he felt a pull around his neck – startling and completely unaccounted for, as if someone was tugging on his leash. He made the trek for the simple reason that he was pulled forward and could come up with no good reason to resist.

Ever since, knowing what awaits him at the top – that is, he thinks he knows, it's all a bit smudged and vague – all his memories are and he really doesn't like digging too deep, it all comes to him when it has to – ever since, he has confidently made his way – up.

The higher he goes, the more unreal everything seems. But he is used to that as well. Except for the stars – now tinged a greenish blue that makes him even more nauseous, nothing here is new to him. That might be the worst part.

The streams run up through the forest in the same old way, glistening unnaturally, not tempting him in the slightest. Not that there's anything to tempt him with – he feels no desire for food or drink, those whiffs that should make his mouth water bring forth fantasies of smashing his nose against the bark of a tree instead. Maybe thirst and hunger are just addictions of sorts. Water and food – just drugs that you learn to do without after a long-enough abstinence. Like months on end in a dark room. That will surely do things to a man's biology, as well as his psyche.

He stomps the thought away. He knows getting to the top will solve all his issues, answer all his questions.

He knows.

It has to.

It takes him a few hours – a day? two? – to reach one of the orbs.

He hates the orbs. He eyes this one from a distance and thinks about all the opinions he has formed over the last five years, the ones that come to him from the abyss of his constantly updating memories. He didn't know he hated the orbs until he saw one. He didn't even know there *were* orbs until he saw one. Yet here it is and he is not surprised by it in the slightest, nor by its artificial appearance – edgeless, perfectly smooth and perfectly balanced. Mocking him.

He knows he will see his own reflection in its surface, if he steps close enough. He knows he doesn't want that. He gives the sphere a wide berth. He puts it out of his mind as soon as he passes it. Maybe he does this every year as well. Isn't it for the best? One should avoid the truth until they are ready to face it. One should not have their fortune read unless they want to know their future.

He does not delve into the past and he does not make guesses about the future. He is a man of the present. That sounds good, much better than admitting that *what was* scares him almost as much as *what will be*. The panic only intensifies when he realizes those two might be the exact same thing. He feels like a fish in a bowl, making the same circle again and again. Someone once told him the point of studying history was to make sure we don't repeat it. He has a feeling he failed history.

He climbs on. The green blurs until his eyes don't even register it as a colour anymore. The solitude suits him just fine. So the ballerina is an unpleasant surprise. Her shoes are a dirty pink.

"You should've stayed in your place."

No memory here. They've never met before. It might be her first year. The rigid way she holds herself tells him that she is uncertain of her circumstances, so he doesn't appreciate the accusatory tone. He is a veteran. He knows what he can and can't do. He has his rights. He thinks. Do lab animals have rights? Certainly. Or they should. Somebody should be fighting for those. He would do it himself but he is terribly busy – he has to get to the top.

Suddenly, he is angry, he really hopes he is a disappointment of an experiment, if that's what he is.

"I'm just passing through."

"You shouldn't. You were placed where you were placed. You will ruin everything."

He is very much ok with that. He doubts he has the power to ruin *everything* but if he can ruin anything at all, he will do so with great pleasure. The thought sends a twinge of guilt through him. He didn't enjoy his journey here. He should have. He was ruining things apparently, he should've been doing so with gusto.

What's the point of ruining anything, if you don't revel in it?

"Unlikely. But, hopefully, I will ruin something."

The ballerina bristles. She is almost frightening now but he seems to have been purged of any dependence on the substance of fear as well. Maybe he was always a brave man.

"You will ruin it all."

"What?"

"The symmetry."

He shakes his head. He has a top to reach. He doesn't have time for this.

And he is almost there. He has made his way so far up that most of the stars are below him now. From here, he can tell that they are truly a mess of colours and he does not like it. He misses the simplicity of the silver glow. If you can't even count on the stars to stay the same, what can you count on? If the stars constantly change, then there is no North Star. If there is no

North Star, then every sailor is always lost. Even if they are to be found by someone, they'll never be able to find themselves. And really, the finding of one's self is the kind of thing that a person should never do via someone else, no matter how convenient it seems.

Why else is he trekking through all this pine once again when it has brought him no true pleasure, when he knows – knows deep inside – what he finds at the top will not make him happy? He didn't even chose this road himself but he is walking it and that must be better than nothing. Better than standing still. If he just stayed where he was put, nothing of what he is would be truly him. This way even his disappointments are his own. Really, they are his own more than anything else.

Up.

Up is better than down. It's just how it is. The same way light is better than darkness. The way strength is better than weakness. The way moving is better than staying still. Untruths that we have made true enough somehow. Through sheer force of repetition.

He moves around a branch and there she is. His disappointments are his own and she is the best one. His angel.

The moment he sees her he feels the change – awareness. The way his arms are steadfastly glued to his sides doesn't feel natural or rather, it feels scarily natural, like they've always been this way. He has always been this way. He is startled by the lightness of the shotgun at his right shoulder – it is infinitely weightless, he couldn't shoot a speck of dust with it, even if he could move his arms. He can't. Now he knows with absolute certainty that he will never be able to take off his coat and hat. Above all, he feels the little wire on top of his head – like a candle's wick. He feels the cap it goes through so it doesn't have to go around his neck. The way hers does.

He moves closer – choppily, stiffly. Moving didn't seem like such an impossible task seconds ago. He is right underneath her now. He can see straight through her – through her glass dress and her glass face, through her glass heart and her glass wings. Those are tinged with gold – the only colour on her. He likes her colourlessness best of all. The wire goes around her neck. Because her glass cap is broken.

He remembers now, of course. He has never seen her cap whole, he has never seen her not hung like this. He makes his pilgrimage to her every year and every year she is just as cold as the one before. Just a pretty ornament. The wire around her neck – just as grotesque. Yet, even broken, she is the right-hand angel – she hangs high up, and he is just a foot soldier. Every year he starts from the bottom and makes his way to her. Every year he reaches her just a few days before… before.

She is the right-hand angel. He looks to the left. Ah, at least this one has not changed. Maybe there is a North Star after all. He wishes he could salute it.

7.

the Story of

In a gothic story she would be "clouded in mystery", in his 21st century reality of caffeine-dependence and self-same days, she is just a creature of habit.

She has exactly one grey beanie, a little frayed at the edge, and exactly one pair of black cut-off gloves that make her fingers look slender and pale. She must be in her early 20's, can't be more than a couple of years older than him, but there's something in the set of her features – a hardness and no-nonsense arrangement of muscles that he associates with a person who has seen many sides of the world and not all of them pretty.

For the last two weeks, she has come in every single day, barely half an hour after he opens. He always stops himself from asking the other baristas if she's here over the weekend as well.

She always orders a cup of tea, sits in the corner furthest from the door and leaves when there's an hour to closing time. She never orders any food and while sometimes she dashes out for a couple of hours around lunchtime it's by no means a rule.

Sometimes he catches sight of a ruffled paperback in her hands. *Oliver Twist* one time, *Peter Pan* the next.

At first he doesn't think much of it, but then, towards the end of that second week, December really makes itself known and her departures start sliding nearer and nearer to closing time. There's apprehension in her eyes and it's not the usual annoyance or reluctance to brave the cold outside the cosy café that he sees on the faces of most patrons during the winter months. Her worry seems almost a physical thing to him, digging its heels into the floor, when she tries to lead it toward the door.

Aileen has been gradually expanding his duties and the first time he's tasked with baking her famous sugar cookies, he makes almost twice as many as he should. He has a *sizable* sweet tooth but he doubts his ability to eat the dozens of extras. So, when she starts zipping up her jacket, which looks like it offers little to no protection from the wind outside, and it's been one of those days when she didn't disappear around lunchtime, he calls out to her without overthinking it.

"Hey, wait!"

He sees her back go ramrod straight and she seems to brace herself before turning around with a painfully fake smile.

"Sorry, I was just wondering if you'd like some sugar cookies?"

Her eyebrows jump up and her smile slips and twists into something that looks very much like suspicion. The seconds tick by and she looks like she is not at all aware that the socially responsible thing to do is answer his question. The awkwardness of the silence slithers up his spine.

"It's just that I made way too much. And Aileen's gonna have my ass for it."

A lie – his boss, bless her soul, won't scold him for anything short of burning the place down. The way his most loyal customer narrows her eyes tells him that she knows that but is choosing not to call him out on it.

"So, yeah, if you wanted some, they're free," he finishes, feeling all kinds of stupid, his fingers curled into a fist at his side.

For her part, she looks way more reluctant than anyone should be about free cookies in his opinion.

"No one who had them today has died yet," he chuckles weakly and starts thinking of a graceful way to back out of the whole interaction (is it an interaction if one of the people is firmly refusing to interact?) when she finally cracks a smile.

He realizes he hasn't seen her smile even once in the last two weeks and yet he never thought her rude or dissatisfied in any way.

"How would you know?"

Her voice has a defensive edge to it but it's loud and clear and there's something playful in her eyes that allows him to laugh lightly.

"Touché."

She gives him this look – makes him feel like he is being quizzed and he sure as hell hasn't studied. It's quite unnerving actually, how at her mercy he feels in those short seconds.

"I can have some cookies," she says with a shrug.

He seems to have passed.

At gingerbread cookies he learns that she has been in New York barely a month and hasn't really explored much, unless you count the interior of his workplace.

At chocolate chip he learns that she likes nothing better than the idea of a white Christmas and yet seems strangely apprehensive at the prospect of actually getting one this year.

At peanut butter he learns that no, she doesn't have any family in town or much in the way of plans for the holidays and she can shut down a conversation with the kind of swiftness and decisiveness that makes him feel ridiculous for even trying to have it.

At glazed lemon he learns that she absolutely cannot stand lemons. Or any citrus fruit for that matter.

At sugar and cinnamon he learns her name.

She exited the café with a bag of cookies just a few minutes ago and he is already locking up and berating himself for feeling like he will miss her over the Christmas weekend, like he will spend Christmas Eve making cookies he's not actually going to eat.

Maybe it's because his mind is still so tangled up in her that he notices her ducking into a small alley across the street. Maybe it's because he knows she'll still be on his mind when he goes to sleep that he follows her.

She gets into an old Desoto and he expects to just watch her drive away with something very akin to disappointment lodged in his breast. Except she doesn't. And, upon closer inspection, it doesn't look like she has been driving much of anywhere recently.

He approaches the car cautiously for reasons he's not entirely sure of and peaks inside. She is sitting in the passenger seat, a blanket on her lap and half a cookie stuffed in her mouth. He starts to smile at the picture she makes before the meaning behind it fully sinks in. Blocks fall into place and fill in the blanks, making sense of this girl that seems less "clouded in mystery" and more simply down on her luck now.

He hesitates for a handful of seconds, takes the time he needs to make sure he knows what he is doing. Usually he trusts the world to back him up and lend a hand if necessary, usually that works just fine for him. It's both daunting and exhilarating to be the one lending a hand. He knocks on her window.

If he didn't feel so guilty for startling her, he would've found the way she jumps, sputtering cookie crumbs all over, highly amusing. But all he feels is contrite as he watches her turn undeniably frightened eyes on him. The fact that her shoulders seem to drop with a relieved sigh when she recognizes him helps a bit.

She hesitates for a solid ten seconds before finally lowering her window. Then she waits and waits and eventually lifts an expectant eyebrow, looking rather exasperated. He can see where that façade cracks though, he can see where she is just as cold as he is and a whole lot more embarrassed.

"Are those your Christmas plans?" he asks and knows it's the wrong thing to say before it has even formed a little cloud in the chilly air.

"I'm sorry if they don't live up to your standards," she grounds out and starts rolling up her window.

"Wait, wait," he reaches to put his hand on the window but decides against it and just lifts his hands in a placating gesture.

She stops the process of shutting him out but takes to regarding him with a mixture of distrust and confusion that seems to do the trick just fine.

"I'm sorry. I didn't mean to be an ass," he says honestly and the self-offense seems to earn him a point or two and the courage to go on. "Most people have trouble starting out here. I know I did."

"Yeah, well," she shrugs and looks down, picking the cookie crumbs off her lap. "I wasn't doing much better before so."

"So, maybe you should let someone help."

Her eyes shoot back up to his and he can't tell if she's mad at him or at herself but she sure doesn't look like she's about to entertain the suggestion.

"Like you?"

"Well… yeah."

She scrutinizes him much like she did the first time he held out a bag of cookies to her. She crosses her arms in front of her chest and gives him an empty smile and he knows he's about to be tested again. And he hasn't studied. Again.

"And what would you suggest helping me with?"

"Not spending Christmas in your car, for starters," he sees no point in beating around the bush and thinks she can hardly get any more defensive.

If her face is anything to go by, he's wrong about that last one. But he swallows and soldiers on.

"So, I can give you some cash for a hotel or the keys to the café."

Her stone cold expression warms a little with surprise. He can't say he blames her. They've emptied the cash register before the holidays but there's still plenty of damage she can do, if she is so inclined. He hardly knows the girl.

Yet he knows his suggestion is in earnest. Aileen might indeed have his head for this one.

"But, honestly? I don't think you want to spend Christmas alone in a hotel room or a dark café, so I think you should come and spend it with me," he finishes, voice surprisingly calm and reasonable.

At least he thinks he sounds reasonable and not at all like he is making a very rash decision, based on his tame life experience and probably more than a little naive belief that most people won't rob you blind or stab you in the back or any of those violent idioms. Reasonable, not heavily influenced by the season of giving and his big sister's voice somewhere behind his right ear, going on about true altruism and how strangers can be the best source of inspiration sometimes.

She seems to waver between bewilderment and amusement.

"And I'm supposed to know that you're not a rapist or a murderer how exactly?"

"How am I supposed to know you aren't?" he fires back.

"You don't. Which is what makes inviting me over for Christmas all the more ridiculous."

He shrugs. He's always thought common sense is overrated. He is confident his sister will be terribly proud, if he makes it out of this without ending up in a hospital or a police station.

"Well, I've decided to worry about that when I wake up on Christmas morning to find that you've stolen all the sugar and cinnamon cookies."

She lifts up the bag in her hand with an unimpressed 'you mean those cookies' expression.

"Please, you think I gave you my whole stash of cookies? I don't like you that much."

For the first time, he thinks she might give his suggestion a thought. He doesn't expect her to open the passenger door and awkwardly shuffle behind the wheel. He frowns in confusion and she finally grins a little.

"You're giving me a place to stay, right?"

He nods.

"Well, I can at least give you a ride there."

He grins back.

Whatever confidence she displayed when accepting his offer

has evaporated by the time she kills her engine and grabs her backpack from the backseat upon his insistence that yes, he is sure about this. She snorts when he offers to carry her luggage and waves jerkily for him to lead the way.

She trails behind him very much like a scolded child but slowing down doesn't bring her into step with him so he has to either let her do her thing or they might just end up stuck in the parking lot, unmoving, with her resolutely two steps behind him. She hesitates again at the door and he lets out a heavy sigh, tossing his keys on the hook by the door and turning to her with his most sincere expression.

"Look, I know I have no way of proving that I'm not an ex-con or something. But I do think the fact that I bake cookies for a living should earn me some points."

She shakes her head and snorts – softer now, less distanced, less distrustful.

"It's not that. I just…" she bites her lip and looks everywhere else before finally bringing her eyes to his. "I've never done the whole Christmas like, properly."

She shrugs, a failed attempt at nonchalance, if he's ever seen one.

"I'm not sure what… how that's done."

"Well, luckily for you, I'm not expecting a visit from the Christmas Inspection Services so I think we can do pretty much whatever we want," he says in a stage whisper that earns him an eyeroll and her finally crossing his threshold.

"Tea?"

"Not a big fan."

"Wha—" he turns from the stove to stare at the woman sitting on his kitchen counter and swinging her feet, inspecting every jar and kitchen towel with what he would consider mock fascination if it wasn't for the genuinely curious expression on her face. "Wait. You don't like tea? I've seen you drink nothing else for the past three weeks."

She shrugs and lowers her eyes to where she's pulling her sleeves down as far as they will go.

"It's the cheapest and warmest."

"Oh."

He waits for her to look up at him but she doesn't. So he moves closer until her still swinging feet are almost kicking his knees.

"So what are you a fan of?"

She finally raises her grey eyes and he swears he's not that full of himself but, for one bizarre second, it seems like she's about to say "you".

"I don't know. Those hot chocolates with the marshmallows inside?"

She shrugs again and he gets the feeling that it's her way of erasing whatever she has said.

He considers her for a second. Knows she's still terribly uncomfortable, knows he risks not finding her in his apartment when he gets back. But it feels like the right thing to do in this moment, like the only next step he can think of.

"I'll be right back. Make yourself at home."

When he returns with all the necessary ingredients for making hot chocolate from scratch, his gamble seems to have paid off. She is snuggled in his armchair, the blanket that he keeps over the back of the couch tucked around her and his copy of *David Copperfield* in her hands. She looks a little sheepish at how well she has executed his suggestion of making herself at home but then he announces his beverage-related plans and she practically runs into the kitchen.

"So, why are you spending Christmas alone?"

"My sister wanted a Christmas honeymoon and my parents decided they've entered the age when they should spend the holiday on a beach. You?"

"My parents decided long ago they've entered the age when they don't give a shit about their kid so… Your friends?"

"Not the friendliest of people."

"Could've fooled me."

"Well, you're just so easy to get along with."

The marshmallow hits him right on the nose.

"So where did you come from?"

"What kind of question is that?"

"Well, you just seem like the kind of person that's… been places."

"What cuz I sleep in my car? Sorry to disappoint but I'm not really some exciting nomad that has stories from every corner of the continent."

"I didn't mean—"

"I mean, I can make up some wild tale about travelling on horseback with a bunch of gypsies or something but—"

"No, that's— You don't have to make stuff up."

"Well, then I'm afraid I'm probably more exciting in your imagination."

"Do we really need more cookies? I thought you had a whole "stash"."

"You might be the worst sous-chef I've ever had."

"Have you ever had a sous-chef?"

"… That's beside the point."

"I don't think I'm any good at this."

"You can't possibly tell already!"

"Why will I ever need to make star-shaped cookies?"

"I don't know. You might want to help out at the café."

"… I don't need you to find me a job."

"You don't?"

"I'm not even any good at this!"

"You don't know that. OK, look, just… forget about that. We're just having fun."

"This is what you do for fun?"

"There is such a thing as humouring your host."

"Never heard of it."

"I'm not taking your bed."

"You're my guest."

"I'm someone you picked off the street."

"So crass. I didn't "pick you", I enticed you into coming over."

"That's creepy."

"And picking someone off the street is the true mark of class?"

"Ugh, just sleep in your bed. Trust me, your couch is a vast improvement on my car. Hell, your bathtub is probably an improvement."

"I don't have a bathtub."

"Excuse me? I'd like to take you up on the hotel room now."

"This is ridiculous."

"Feel free to go to bed at any time."

"We haven't known each other that long but I can assure you that I'm more stubborn than you."

"You just proved that we haven't known each other that long."

"Alright. What if we are equally stubborn and end up spending the night on the couch with an empty bed ten feet away?"

"That would be stupid."

"Precisely."

"So you should go to bed. "

"For the love of—"

"How's your neck?"
"Same as yours I'm guessing."
"Shut up."

They go to the store for more chocolate to melt into hot cocoa and buy ungodly amounts of marshmallows like the legal adults they are. A couple of years ago he might have felt guilty – like he was cheating at life or something. Then, slowly but surely, it was brought to his attention that nobody knows what they are doing when it comes to life – not his teachers, not his big sister, not his boss, not even his parents. Everybody is just winging it. Everybody will forever feel more connected to that chocolate-dipped marshmallow candy they used to love as a child than to any healthy and nutritious meal they master in their own kitchen, in their own apartment, cooking for their sophisticated friends. They will forever be more connected to their favourite cartoon than to any inspiring successful person's autobiography that they read in their 30's, turning the pages with slight desperation, looking for what they have been missing. Forever connected to the child they used to be more than the adult they are trying to be and inexplicably ashamed of that.

He watches her run down the empty aisle with their shopping cart, gaining momentum, lifting her feet up half way and letting it carry her all the way to the powdered sugar. He is not often ashamed of being more connected to the child than the adult – not anymore, but in that moment it still feels like too often. And, even as he pushes the cart forward and lifts his legs that little bit too soon and feels the point of balance slip past him and away, even as he falls flat on his back and drags the cart along with him, even as he hears her running toward him with something like panic in her voice – the kid inside can't stop laughing. Maybe every time he laughs, it's that kid coming to the surface. He lets her help him up and he extends his hand and introduces himself again as if they've just met.

And that's pretty much the story of how she hugs him for the first time.

He can manoeuvre in his kitchen with his eyes closed at this point.

So the way her sweater slips down, exposing her shoulder and the grey strap of her bra, the way she keeps tucking away the strands of hair that escape her braid, the way her laugh fills the space between them when she puts a spoon under the water spray and it splashes her in the face, the way she grabs his arm to steady herself as she slips on the little puddle on the floor – those are the things he blames his absent-mindedness on.

His hiss and subsequent curses are much less amusing than her delightful laughter but she just grabs his non-burned hand and leads him into the bathroom and takes out his first aid kit.

And that's pretty much the story of how she holds his hand for the first time.

They eat more than any two humans should no matter what

holiday it is.

But there is just something so liberating about it. It's the holidays, have another cookie. It's the holidays, have another cup of mulled wine. It's the holidays, spend those extra few bucks. It's the holidays, put on that album you pretend to hate. It's the holidays, ask the mysterious girl from the café to spend them with you.

He has always been a 'in for a penny, in for a pound' kind of guy. So they watch *Love Actually* as he systematically bites off the heads of all their gingerbread men and she digs out a Santa hat along with his two sets of twinkling lights.

She also brings out his guitar. She tells him the whole 'girls are so into musicians' thing is no joke, asks if he still remembers any songs and upon his nod, asks if maybe he could teach her some, asks if guys are into musicians as well. He doesn't know really, supposes he'll be into lumberjacks as well, if she put on some flannel and started swinging an axe.

And that's pretty much the story of how she kisses him for the first time.

They decide that, since they fell asleep on the couch together, they can fall asleep in bed together as well.

They only wake up when the sun is high in the sky, its rays bouncing off the snow-covered rooftops outside. She jumps out of bed and stumbles to the window, squishing her nose against it in a way that does something terrifying to his heart. And she's wearing a flannel shirt, and her hair is a mess, and she fogs the window pane with his name, and tells him they're having a white Christmas, as if he's not currently half-blinded by the damn snow and half by the joy of her. And when she turns around, he's sure all those terrifying things happening to his heart are written all over his face. They can't scare her too much though, if she slips back between the covers.

And that's pretty much the story of how she stays.

8.
Is It Serendipity
(or am I just a bad penny?)

The first time he meets her she is loud and sharp and irritable, and that's coming from the guy in the ER on Christmas Eve with a bone protruding from his leg. She is barking out orders left, right and centre, and part of him is admiring the way she plants her feet and makes the world turn around her. The rest of him wants to roll his eyes at all the noise that's being made over his foolishness. She has no bedside manner to speak of and barely raises an eyebrow when he tries to sweet-talk his way into some extra pain meds and maybe seeing what her smile looks like. That doesn't seem very likely from where he is lying right now. But her jade eyes are truly something else – adrenaline-wide, unnecessary anxious and so full he feels like there are more stories inside her than in his grandfather's library. He wants to ask her to slow down for a moment, to give him a chance to inspect all the spots and flecks in her irises. He is starting to feel inexplicably and progressively lost as she sets about putting his bones to rights, time seems to stretch and distort in a way that he hopes can be blamed on the meds, and he tries to anchor himself in his doctor's steely gaze.

The second time he is there to have his cast removed and still aching all over. He sees her hurrying through the waiting room – a flash of life among the deadening fluorescent lights, a blur of blue among the greys and dirty whites, which he thinks must be the same thing. He immediately tries to straighten up from his slouched position in the less-than-comfortable plastic chair. He thinks she catches sight of him and slows her step for a millisecond. But then he always did have an overactive imagination.

The third time hardly counts because he remembers her face hours after the almost-encounter. He storms out of the coffee shop that's in no way in his neighbourhood, in a rush to get somewhere and armed only with the vague directions of his one-night stand and the biggest Americano they could make. She trudges into the coffee shop that's only two blocks from her apartment, barely keeping her eyes open and feeling the pressure and invisible filth of a 27-hour shift. And he barely glances at her and she has her gaze glued to her shoes and they don't crash into each other and he only remembers who she is when his headache finally lets up a bit, and it's a day like any other – cheated out of its possibility.

The fourth time he sees her at a Florence + the Machine

concert. And this time she does crash into him, spilling something horribly red on his left sleeve and muttering something that might be an apology as she surges on through the crowd. He tries to stop her, talk to her, jog her memory, he tries to move in some way that doesn't feel stiff and inadequate. She either doesn't hear him shouting after her or she is terribly good at ignoring people. Or maybe he never made a sound after all. He wants to follow her, reach out and grab her arm, but he is way too aware of the possibility of her turning around and him ending up with another broken bone, so he lets her get swallowed up by the pressing mass of people that is pushing him this way and that and making him feel like he is adrift at sea and just lost sight of the shore.

The fifth time he sees her on a screen. There must have been some accident. She snaps at a journalist that she has better things to do than stand around and *talk* about the people she is meant to be helping. Her ponytail is a study in disaster, her collarbone stands out in sharp relief and its fragility makes his own itch uncomfortably beneath his skin. There's something that looks a lot like blood at the end of her sleeve and her face is set in a scowl, but her eyes still give him a glimpse into tomes upon tomes that he would like to explore and he tries to exercise powers he doesn't have to keep her image in front of him, but she is gone before he can so much as memorize the way she grits her teeth and squares her shoulders. The sway of her ponytail is uncannily ominous and he feels like he is watching the pendulum of his life's clock, counting down time he doesn't have.

The sixth time he is there for a burn. He can't quite recall how it all happened. It's nothing serious but it stings and pulls mercilessly at his nerve endings and the pain seems to go below and beyond his flesh. She is clearly exhausted, the kind of exhausted that looks like she's having trouble carrying her very bones around, the kind that dims the sparkle in her eyes. He doesn't know what time it is but it must be near the end of her shift – he hopes it is. Her movements are sluggish and delayed, her gaze almost apologetic. So he stays quiet and only gives her a smile of thanks when she is done wrapping his hand, and she doesn't smile back but her nod looks something like grateful.

The seventh time it's Christmas Eve again. His younger brother is running a fever. His parents must be truly panicked to take him to the ER. The sense of apprehension weighs on his spine so heavy that he barely spares a thought for the doctor whose eyes have an almost hypnotizing effect on him. It's probably for the best, he needs to stay focused, he needs to clear his head, the drowsiness and panic are battling for control over his eyelids. But she is the one on shift once again and her jarred edges soften around his brother and his soft brown eyes. She is almost nice to the poor kid and very professional in front of his parents but she doesn't so much as glance in his direction and he just doesn't have the strength to draw her attention – too busy fighting the worry that has settled bone-deep.

The eighth time he knows his wrist is barely sprained. He is in no need of emergency care but those damn eyes of hers have power of attraction stronger than anything he could attempt to resist right now. They drag at his mind, at his whole damn skeleton. Thinking about it, he might have done his wrist in on purpose. Subconsciously. Just for a glimpse of that shade of green which reminds him of the ocean toward the end of summer – turbulent and no longer certain of its colour. And then she is not there, of course. Well, she is, but how is he to know that she is taking a nap on a bumpy cot with a cooled cup of coffee by her side not a hundred meters from him? He can't know, not really.

The ninth time doesn't count either. She is in her car and he is crossing the street and he can say he feels a pair of eyes on his back and he can say that a shiver runs down the twisted length of his spine, reverberating through his ribs, rattling the cage around his heart and settling somewhere in his low back, a bone that he does not know the name of vibrating plaintively. But he can't say what colour those eyes are, can't say if they are assessing him with interest or worry, if they belong to his guardian angel or a driver in a hurry, annoyed with his slow, hungover ways.

The tenth time he is not there to see the wife of one of his co-workers regaling the doctor with the emerald eyes with the story of their frankly ridiculous trip to Disneyland. He is not there when she goes to shake her head at the offer to join their next shindig. He is not there when those eyes of hers land on his face among the crowd in the photo. He is not there when her voice catches but she powers through her refusal.

The eleventh time he thinks he must be dreaming because it is literally perfect. She is sitting at a table in one of the smallest bistros in town and her hair is pulled into a messy but rather fetching bun and her eyes are shining that little bit brighter, perhaps thanks to the glass of wine by her hand, and she is alone, if the book in her other hand is any indication (*Dubliners*, he files away) and she is wearing a soft blue dress and a deep red scarf and she looks up when he walks in and her lips twitch in something almost, *almost* like the smile that he so desperately wanted to see that first time. It's perfect. Except for the bubbly brunette that has a painful grip on his arm. His doctor asks for the bill the second they sit down and he can't recall anything after she walks out.

The twelfth time he walks into the ER on Christmas Eve, two years after looking her in the eyes for the first time. No broken bones, no burns, just a thermos of coffee in one hand, a bag of snowflake-shaped cookies in the other and a spring of mistletoe in his back pocket. He waits for two hours, letting confused strangers with actual injuries go in before him, bouncing his leg and biting his nails, and losing half his cookies to little kids with big eyes. When he is finally the only 'patient' left, he walks in and feels a small wave of excitement hit him when he sees the red waves spilling over her back. It was a bit of a gamble but he has a feeling she takes a lot of shifts around the holidays.

He wants to reach out for her, he has a speech ready and everything. He knows she'll say something about landing himself in the ER way too often, knows it's probably becoming suspicious. Sometimes he feels like an elastic band – no matter how far he goes, he is always pulled back here. Back to her. He wishes he could tether himself to her somehow, wishes she would turn around so he can ground himself in her eyes.

He has a joke ready – about an evil witch placing a Christmas curse on him. He vows not to say something corny about how she has certainly put him under her spell.

Since he met her, he has entertained the idea of serendipity way too often. As well as the fact that she probably sees him more as a bad penny.

It's unnerving and exhilarating all at once – she is right there and she has yet to look at him – he feels his heartrate spike and the blood rushing through his veins sounds especially loud and he swears his bones are tingling. If she would just turn around, he'd like to try and put it all into words.

But she doesn't. She keeps her back to him, putting things away, lightly shaking her takeout cup to see if there's anything left inside. He clears his throat, takes a deep breath, prepares for those damn eyes and the surprise and possible exasperation.

She still doesn't turn. He frowns. Does she know it's him? Is she ignoring him on purpose? He raps his knuckles against the doorframe.

IS IT SERENDIPITY (OR AM I JUST A BAD PENNY?)

Fuck. That hurts. From his tender skin, all the way to his very marrow – the little action reverberates through his whole being and just like that he feels each and every bone that is not in its right place.

Fuck.

It's Christmas Eve and he has more than one bone protruding from his body. He blinks – once, twice, thrice before she comes into focus. Her eyes are still green. They don't know him. He lets his own slip closed and prays he gets to meet her a second time.

9.

Tea, Toy Trains & Other Necessities

She is still at the start of her seven-year shift and already at the end of her proverbial rope. Matthew Kelly (27 out of 88, disaster level 7, dumb luck level 5) might just turn out to be the human that makes her switch career paths.

"Bloody America!"

She groans. Perhaps a bit too loudly, considering the looks three separate people throw her way, but she doesn't care. She has been listening to this man moan and groan, mutter and grumble under his breath about "Bloody America" and "centre of commercialism, HA" and "disorganized Yanks" for a week now.

Disorganized? Really, Kelly? Really?

She desperately wants to ignore him but, if the last 5 months have taught her anything, it's that she cannot watch this guy struggle. (And he sure is good at struggling.) It must be some kind of built-in detector that makes sure she does her job properly. It gnaws at her, does something irritating as all hell to her stomach and general chest area and basically doesn't leave her be until he is back to his naturally lost (not 'impending doom' lost) state.

Before she came down, she was told the guy is a great artist (something about hanging in the MET in 20 years), a royal pain in the ass and the kind of friend that will save everybody's skin before his own when it came down to it. A recipe for disaster. Exactly the kind bound to find its way to her desk. Her success rate with artists is not 86% for nothing.

However, she was not told that he is the most disorganized person she has ever had to watch over, the creature with the worst self-preservation skills on the planet and probably the human result of a hurricane mating with a tornado.

Truly, she specialized in creative souls, she has seen some absent-minded shit (to the point where she once requested a check-up to make sure the girl actually *had* a mind) but this is like observing a whole new kind of species. There are only so many times you can watch someone almost staple their own hand by accident. How he still has all ten fingers is a mystery to her. Why he insists on using a stapler in the second decade of the 21st century is another.

So, knowing her wrist (that particular spot that seems to be a 'Kelly is in trouble' button now) is going to itch all day and well into the night, if she doesn't at least try to help him, she decides to just bite the bullet. Nonchalantly, of course.

"What has the country that took you in and gave you a job done wrong this time?"

"I'll have you know, I can head back and get the same job on the other side of the planet."

Which will probably terminate her contract and make her life a lot easier and calmer and quieter and, generally, will suck. But no one needs to dwell on the whens and whys of that.

"And yet, here you are. So what have the "Yanks" done to offend your Irish sensibilities this time?"

"For a country that prides itself on having completely dehumanized and commercialized the Christmas holiday, you sure make it difficult for a man to do a spot of Christmas shopping," he sighs and, after a few more angry hits at his keyboard, pushes his chair away from the desk and leans his head back with a groan of defeat.

She doesn't stare at the muscles in his neck, the veins and the Adam apple and all that. Kelly is a big fan of the whole God-why-me, eyes-to-the-ceiling, head-thrown-back, hands-behind-your-neck thing. She knows better than to look. She also knows it's not upwards he should be looking.

"First of all, we don't exactly *pride* ourselves on it. It just… happened," she thinks so at least – her own citizenship has been less than properly acquired and she doesn't feel like she has got the hang of being American just yet (she misses Europe, even though her last case was an absolute bastard that she maintains shouldn't have qualified at all). "Second, what the hell are you looking for?"

"A toy train, Miss Devine. A mere classical, well-functioning, realistic-looking toy train."

She can't help it. She looks. And, yeah, he makes as sinful a picture as she imagined he would.

"Why are you looking for a toy train?"

She knows this will not be a life-altering purchase – he might make it, he might not. As a matter of fact, nothing crucial to the grand scheme of things or his own life will be happening to Matthew Kelly until next year.

"Well," he has the decency to roll his chair so he can incline his head to the side and look at her without actually regaining use of his neck muscles just yet. "My sister and her wife are so kind as to drag themselves all the way across the ocean to spend the holidays with me. Least I can do is buy them and my nephews decent gifts now, isn't it?"

There are things about Matthew Kelly that make her scrunch up her nose in honest confusion. Not only normal human things that she finds naturally distasteful but very specific ones that she is trying not to be even remotely charmed by.

Like how he puts more milk in his tea than actual water and won't drink any at all, if *someone* doesn't replace the carton in the office kitchen every week. And how he can go without water for 8 hours straight, if *someone* doesn't throw a water bottle at his head. And how he'll create a piece of artwork and then completely forget to submit it to their boss for approval unless *someone* exclaims (loudly and repeatedly) how they have only an hour to go before they are done for the day, only half an hour now, better start tidying up, twenty minutes and *boy, she hopes she sent in all her projects*!

And then there are other things. Like how he urges her to play her music even when she's forgotten her headphones (she just can't get used to those, can't get rid of the nagging feeling that they will bump into the other accessory over her head that's not really there right now) because surely no one would mind being treated to her excellent taste in punk rock bands. And how he brings donuts for the whole office and comes to her first so she can snag the lemon glaze one. And how he answers passive-aggressive emails in a way that drives everybody up the wall because they don't realize that his passive-aggressive radar is completely non-existent. She knows, she asked for a check-up.

And then there are yet other things. Like how, whenever he talks about his sister, she doesn't get the annoying, empty feeling she gets whenever other people talk about siblings and family and mortal connections like that, but instead feels curious and warm all over.

She is pretty good at keeping all those irrelevant things to herself. She is not that good at staying out of his business even when it doesn't really fall within the parameters of her business.

"Are you being a lazy ass and trying to find one online?"

He finally straightens. If just to glare at her.

"It's called availing myself of the modern comforts that are supposed to compensate us for the pollution of our planet, love."

He is not wrong but she is half-convinced he says those things simply to see if her eyes can roll out of her head.

"Sure, Mr. 'I can't work with Excel, Lena! Rescue me from these task sheets! I'm a creative soul, Lena! This is killing everything good and pure inside me!'"

He looks at her long and hard and then sighs in something reminiscent of resignation.

"At least you didn't do the accent."

"You just gotta go out there and do the leg work, like any other tortured soul caught in the pre-holiday madness," she says with a shrug before turning back to her computer.

"Must I?"

She doesn't look at the pout and the lashes and the baby blues. She knows better. But she hears it all in his all-suffering sigh just the same.

You sent me into the lion's den, Devine! The pit of hell!

She panics for a second, thinking that she did somehow do that, which is ridiculous and impossible and—

And for naught!

Attached is a selfie of one Matthew Kelly with a perfectly satisfactory toy train in the background, which has apparently failed to meet his standards, if his face is anything to go by.

She doesn't reply. But 20 minutes later she opens her laptop and starts a toy train search that, combined with the unspeakably frustrating limitations of the human knowledge and ability to acquire such only bit by tiniest bit, takes her well into dinner.

Step 1 is putting him on the mailing list for the online shop in which (at 2 am, Heaven help her, she doesn't understand how humans get anything done with so few hours in a day and brains that need so many of those hours to process a miniscule amount of information) she finally found a train set so intricate and decadent even Kelly will have to be impressed. She has little hope of that being enough. He hardly checks his mail, let alone clean out his Spam folders or open adverts.

Step 2 is an extraordinary amount of pointed hints to maybe look online again, maybe try a few stores known for their handmade toys, maybe this or maybe that. She should've known better. The man continues to be foiled by technology at every turn.

Step 3 is literally leaving a post-it with the shop's name on his desk.

That desk is a whole other nightmare (and a potential biohazard) and her post-it doesn't even have the chance to get the trademark Kelly teacup ring on it before it is lost under an avalanche of sketches, napkins, torn sheets of paper and other equally doomed post-its.

She is well-aware that the logical next step is to just tell him where he can find the stupid train, say she stumbled upon it by accident and be done with it. But that is not how they do things in this business. Well, it could be, but those cheat methods are for suckers and she is a professional.

And listen, it's not like he is her favourite human or anything.

He is laughably flirty and stupidly confident, he has the attention span of a six-year-old and he eats too much candy and leaves the wrappers everywhere, he overuses the cobalt blue and always picks the most obscure fonts to work with, his dimples are really noticeable, he drums his fingers over the buttons when he rides the elevator, his hair always looks good, he holds the door for everyone and their dog, he either leaves all the windows open and soon papers are flying everywhere or he cranks up the AC until she is dripping sweat over her keyboard, he is obnoxious and scatter-minded and really attractive, he has a pretty great voice which he unfortunately uses to start singing Christmas carols the second Halloween is out the door, he is the kind of person who picks the most pathetic-looking tree for the office and then spends two hours and forty-five minutes straightening its branches and picking out just the right ornaments that won't make it stoop too much, he forgets to turn off his computer three days out of the work week and he is clueless when it comes to office drama and he is way too into STAR WARS and his laughter is like, seriously loud, he calls slush and three snowflakes every 15 minutes "wonderful weather", he is too competitive and too honest and too… Irish.

He is most definitely her favourite human. So maybe she goes a bit overboard sometimes but honestly, what's the harm? Since when is working overtime a sin? (It's not, she knows the Sins catalogue by heart.)

Supplying the office kitchenette with drinks and snacks is not in the catalogue. Their office manager used to do that but she also used to get this tea that Kelly dubbed "undrinkable" and, after trying three different brands, the girl finally gave up and told him to lower his tea standards. And look, they talk, ok? How is she to know what tinkering is needed in his life, if she doesn't know what's going on in said life? So she happens to know his favourite podcasts and his favourite superheroes and his favourite pizza toppings and his favourite tea brands. She also happens to know where they sell those. About half way across town. So naturally she has taken to supplying the kitchen cabinets.

Supplying the office with stationery is also not in the catalogue. See, Kelly is left-handed and he'll joke around and complain about every little thing just to be a pain but he would never actually ask anyone to buy left-handed scissors just for him. So she had to take over stationery and, naturally, pretend she bought left-handed scissors by mistake (as well as those colourful paper clips that he claims make everything much easier and "cheerier").

She also happens to be the one that turns off his computer three days out of the work week.

And the one who orders food for the whole office when it's 3 pm and he has yet to eat anything.

And the one who last Wednesday snuck around to his desk to retrieve his lost file after he took a break from swearing at his computer and went to make himself a cup of tea.

And the one who in October hid a beanie in his laptop bag, whose origins he tried to puzzle out for a week before the temperatures really dropped and he just started wearing it.

And the point is that if she stops doing stuff for him, she is not sure how long he will last, ok? And none of it is in the catalogue so it's not like she's doing anything wrong. It's not like she enjoys it. Much. It's her job. Kind of. She is putting in some extra hours. It will look good on her CV.

The 22nd is their last day at work before the holidays and Kelly looks dejected at best when asked how his shopping went. He shrugs, mutters something about board games being all the rage this season and tries to construct a smile from the crumbs of his frown still clinging to his mouth.

She has just made herself a cup of coffee to carry her through the last two hours of the workday when he flies past her – his scarf and hair in the usual disarray and his smile and "Happy Holidays" a little more genuine now as he meets her eye.

Her desk – unlike other people's – is orderly to a fault, downright Spartan, if you ask Kelly. Which makes it all too easy for her to spot the little red box and the freaking post-it as soon as she takes her seat.

'Hopefully some of my shopping endeavours were successful'

It's a beautiful glass angel with golden tipped wings. For a few seconds, she just stops breathing, her vision sharpens painfully, her back starts itching unbearably – those two lines along her shoulder blades. Then she exhales and shakes her head.

Nonsense. The man wouldn't know a meteor, if it fell from the sky and landed at his feet.

"Yes?" Matt practically growls as he wrenches his door open and tries not to glower at the clearly lost delivery boy in front of him.

He has 5 hours before he has to pick his sister from the airport and his apartment… is not exactly guests-ready. (He needs to set aside at least an extra hour for getting there – he always takes a wrong turn on the way to the bloody airport.)

"A delivery from The Rabbit Hole Toy Store."

"I'm sorry, I believe you have the wrong address, mate," he answers with a frown, while mentally putting more and more objects on his grocery list – he should probably write it down, he has already forgotten the first four items.

"Matthew Kelly?"

"Yeah."

"Then this is for you, sir."

The boy reaches over to drag a huge brown package that was leaning against the wall.

"I did not order this," he reaches to help despite his confusion and growing annoyance.

"Well, maybe your Secret Santa did," the teenager mutters without too much cheer. "It's paid for and you just have to sign here."

Brow furrowed in bewilderment, brain working overtime to figure out if he could have ordered and paid for something from a store he has never even heard of, he signs the slip of paper and watches the boy run down the stairs before he shakes his head and closes the door. He rips into the paper with barely a moment of hesitation.

"Bugger me!"

Matthew Kelly is not a non-believer. Christmas miracles are a real thing as far as he is concerned. And he is pretty confident that his is a control freak with a coffee addiction, an aversion to headphones and a deep love for the Sex Pistols.

And will deny it into next Christmas.

10.

In December
(we move on)

They meet in March. He – a blur of blue flannel and flying frisbees, fresh off the rig and unshaven, beer on his breath and exhilaration in his veins, bright-eyed, 26 and on top of the bloody world, cursing Dan for the awkward throw and reaching his arm out as far as it will go. She – an adorable mess of tangled limbs and black curls, lips chapped and pink and pulled back in a snarl, coffee spilled all over her white sweater and eyes flashing in anger, cursing him for not looking where he was literally throwing himself and rebuffing all of his apologies and offers to buy her another drink and pay for her dry-cleaning.

They have dinner in April. He – a combination of trembling insides and nonchalant poses, hair refusing to remain in its carefully chosen and executed arrangement, twirling the single sunflower in his hand round and round just so he doesn't constantly check his damn phone, praying to every deity out there that he doesn't blow his chance after frequenting her preferred coffee shop and working his blasted charms on her for weeks. She – a vision in silver, all teasing smiles and playful scowls, telling him not to spill anything on her 'cause that's her favourite dress, stealing food off his plate and nudging hers toward him, swiping the chocolate in the corner of her mouth and licking her thumb without the slightest clue about the silent roars inside him, taking his hand to lead him down the street when they exit the restaurant minutes before closing time, slipping her fingers between his instead of putting on her gloves.

They go sailing in June. He – a picture of ease and confidence, feet planted firmly on the deck of his small boat, carefree and proud, in his element and determined to show off shamelessly, enchanted by the stubborn way her hair keeps blowing in her face and the unreserved way she jumps and squeals in delight whenever the spray reaches her flushed cheeks, tugging at the ends of her sleeve to tip her into his lap, murmuring praises and promises against the hollow of her throat. She – a study in contentment, sunglasses perched low on her sunscreen-smeared nose, a smile full of wonder and unadulterated joy permanently etched on her face, pointing at every single object on deck and asking him what it is and what it is for, sneaking her arms around him and butting her nose between his shoulder blades, peppering his neck with kisses and breathing life to words he has been holding back all day.

They meet the family in July. He – a personification of cool and collected, employing every single shred of charm and wit he possesses to combat her father's frigid stare, keeping his arm obviously but not possessively wrapped around her shoulders, soaking up every high school story her mom volunteers and laughing until her elbow almost bruises one of his ribs, falling more and more in love with the rose colour high on her cheeks and the way she buries her face in his shoulder. She – a vibrating and irritable exposed wire, as much of a nervous wreck as he has ever seen her, shaking his grandfather's hand firmly with a crooked smile that won't pick a corner of her month in which to settle, letting out a little yelp as the old man pulls her into a hug, smiling at him with what she will most assuredly deny but are obviously tears in her eyes.

He ships out in October. A confusing mix of muscles aching for some hard work and heart aching at the thought of being away from her, kissing each of her knuckles and promising to call her every day, bunching up her sweater in his grip and murmuring in her ear about visiting her dreams every night. She – a heart-wrenching picture of control and vulnerability, shining eyes and arms squeezing him so hard he thinks (hopes) he'll have bruises later, a trembling smile pressed against every inch of his face, words of present frustration and future patience.

He returns in November. A broken mess of a man, plus a hefty compensation, minus a leg and the conviction that made him set foot on an oil rig, still aching for her with the most vital parts of him and pulling away with all the same parts – twisted and scarred like the rest of him, brushing only her very fingertips when she tries to hold his hand, flinching away completely when she reaches for the bandages below his knee, occasionally avoiding phone calls and missing therapy sessions and generally drinking more than he should, going over every argument (that he ignored for years) against the work he used to put his whole being into and focusing on every little detail that clicked into place so fate could punish him for it, brooding and overthinking her absence when she is gone and rejecting and rationalizing her presence when she is around, hanging up and throwing his phone across the room at the first word of defence for the company from his grandfather, picking fights just to see how far he can push before she snaps and gives up on him. She – a beam of light in the darkness that he tries to shield his disillusioned and red-rimmed eyes from despite the pleas of his heart, a force of nature trying to pull him back to her and then trying to hide her hurt when he remains as far emotionally as he has been physically for the last month, giving him space to come back on his own and then storming every defence he has carefully put up against the world when he doesn't, refusing to let him hide in his apartment for more than three days in a row and refusing to rise to his constant baits and refusing to give up on him and generally making his heart even more of a mess than it already is.

It all comes to a head in December.

He grinds his teeth and listens to her go on about how it's going to be small and private and how her father has already invited his grandfather and he has accepted and that means if he keeps trying to wiggle out of it, she will call them both and gang up on him. And he's been ignoring his grandfather and don't even get her started on their friends. And he is about to snap and ask if they wouldn't prefer to get together and just talk about him all night instead of have him there. But then she sighs on the other side and it sounds exhausted and so damn stubborn and he just can't keep doing this to her, not like this – half-assed and mean and never pulling far enough to break the string he seems to have tied them together with. So he decides to play a long game, a long game of crushing every bit of possibility left. He says he'll go, says he'll pick her up at 6, asks her to wear the silver dress and digs his nails into his palm and bites down on his tongue and hates himself for it.

He manages to avoid her the two days before the party, snapping out his refusals when she asks to come to his physiotherapist and citing Christmas shopping that she obviously can't do with him unless she wants to ruin his surprise.

The rub is that he actually does go shopping – from the dubious comfort of his couch and with the sole help of his internet provider but still – and he does buy her that gift he never intends to give her. He clicks through the user-friendly interface and immerses himself in the illusion that he is just another guy, avoiding the jostling holiday crowds and purchasing a gift for his significant other online.

Maybe he plays pretend a bit too well because for that one

moment, as he sits on the couch and for once sips tea instead of bourbon, he forgets. He forgets it's all an illusion. Then the little red light comes on and he goes to get his changer and loses his balance.

The 24th unfolds with one missed call and two gently probing texts that go unanswered. He sits with good old Mr. Scrooge in his hand, giving him a run for his money in the bastard category, and watches the clock in the corner of his screen move from 6:00 to 6:06 to 6:10 to 6:17 to 6:21 to 6:30 because apparently he likes feeling every little bit of happiness in his heart burn out, crumble to ash and seep down into his heel.

Half a year ago he would've said Lexi Jones is the single most impatient woman he has ever had the pleasure of knowing and won't wait for anything but a delivery from her very favourite pizza place for more than 10 minutes. Over the last month, he has learned that Lexi Jones has the patience and restraint of a saint, the ability to duck under all his snide comments and nasty jokes and reach him, tangle her hands in his hair and press her lips to his brow and make him shut his fucking mouth for a few seconds and remember what not doubting everything he's ever known about life and himself feels like. But, as he looks at his silent phone, he thinks this – this is pushing it even for her, and then, for a moment, he thinks she never expected him to show up at all, for a second – that is equal parts relief and utter despair – he considers the possibility that she never wanted him to.

And then there's a knock on his door. One he resolutely ignores.

"I do have a key, you know? This is just a courtesy knock."

His right leg starts bouncing in agitation and he squeezes the glass in his hand tighter but stubbornly refuses to twitch another muscle. His door opens seconds later.

He doesn't turn around but soon enough she is standing before him in all her enraged glory. That damn silver dress is shimmering over her hips like it's made of pure magic and her lips are painted a deep red that makes his heart speed up even pressed as they are into a thin, unamused line. Her hair is curled the way it was when he first literally crashed into her and he notes that she has let it grow really long this time, wonders if it's intentional, wonders if she knows how much he loves it like that since he has never told her. Her fists on her hips do nothing to take away from her elegance and everything to spike up his raging desire to grab her and pull her into him.

"So I take it we're not going to the party?"

He is in his sweatpants, hasn't showered since yesterday and is just another two drinks away from nicely buzzed. Two drinks he's suddenly desperate to get to.

"Why, darling? Are you not feeling festive?"

He takes a sip and gives her a dark look for making him do this in person, for not being a coward like him and just letting them slip into oblivion the way he has been trying to ever since he got back and fighting her every step of the way.

"Honestly? No. What I'm feeling is confused," she states before her voice softens impossibly and he can't look her in the eyes anymore, not when the anger seeps out of them so quickly. "Will, if you didn't want to go to the party, you could've just told me so."

"Oh, could I? 'Cause you seemed pretty set on dragging me to it a couple days ago."

"I thought you'd enjoy it! I thought you'd enjoy being out. Around people. You haven't seen your grandfather in a week!"

"You two seem to keep each other updated," he grits out and downs his drink.

He scowls at the empty glass, already regrets taking his temporary prosthetic off. It bothers him – partly on a purely physical level and partly— His doctor assured him that his permanent one would feel much more comfortable and natural, grinning at him as if he was talking about a fucking sports car that he'll be taking for a spin.

"Look," she clenches her jaw and he feels an ounce of victory at managing to rile her up again. "I'm trying to figure out what you want here but you're not giving me much. Is this how you want us to spend our first Christmas?"

First. It pierces him – fast and fierce, and he feels his shoulders sag as he leans his head back to stare at the neutral ceiling instead of her flashing eyes or the way the light bounces off his glass – it's a contest which one is glaring at him with more accusations.

"No, I wanted some goddamn peace and quiet," he mutters

and sees her flinch from the corner of his eye, tries with every bit of willpower left inside him to leave it at that, to not yield an inch, and fails when she doesn't budge from her spot. "And I wanted you to go and have a nice Christmas with people who can give you that."

"They can't give me that. They can't give me you."

He laughs mirthlessly, looks at her, spreads his arms wide.

"And I'm all you want for Christmas, right?"

It's as sarcastic as anything he has ever said and he curses the small part inside him that says that's all he wants, curses even more foully the even smaller part that still believes it's all she wants as well.

"No," she grits out and he lets his arms drop, tries and tries and fails to school his features into a mockingly shocked expression.

But then she charges forward and there's only a split second between him realizing what she is doing and her crashing into his lap – her knees sinking into the couch cushions on either side of him. He doesn't do much as she grabs his faded t-shirt and pulls him into her, lips harsh and punishing, biting at his bottom lip viciously, her hands pounding his chest hard enough to sting but not hard enough to push him away from her, furious and stubborn until she's not. Until her hands slide up his neck and cradle his face, her lips releasing the tiniest sob that still makes him feel like the worst criminal in the world, abandoning his mouth to spread haphazard kisses everywhere she can reach.

It's so much like the time she sent him off to his ultimate

failure and disillusionment and yet nothing like it. She was trembling then, now she is unyielding, hopeful before, now forceful, determined. She didn't tell him not to leave then but she is set on making him come back now.

She pulls away and drops her forehead against his. Hard. And again. And again. Until he is convinced she wants to see which one of them will get knocked out first.

He grabs her shoulders and pushes her away, just enough to look her in the eyes. The multitude of colours inside them are painfully visible from this close. He can see each and every one and it makes him realize how long it's been since he had her so near. He kisses her again. Just this one more time.

Her forehead finally comes to rest against his, pressing into his skin almost aggressively, her left hand stills on his cheek and her right one squeezes his thigh only hard enough for him to know she is conscious of the scars there, her breath is warm on his face and her nose is surprisingly cold against his own.

"You're not all I want for Christmas, you fucking idiot."

She sounds enraged at the mere suggestion and it makes his brows bunch up in confusion. Because she might say she doesn't want him but he is pretty sure she'll growl and bite at him if he tries to move even half an inch away.

"You're all I want, period."

Ah.

He risks that half an inch, pulls back only to descend on her lips again. He has heard the sound she makes a few times, they always argue whether or not it's a meow but he is positive there is no other way to describe it. His lips slant over her cheek, ungraceful kisses, beard burn and wet spots all he leaves behind as he treks the path to her neck. She moves closer – as close as another human can possibly get without taking her clothes off, and he remembers what it's like when she does, remembers it vividly. But they haven't— Not since—

He drops his forehead on her shoulder and feels her fingers dig lightly into his scalp. He doesn't know if he can bear to taint what they had with what they can have now, with something… less.

"Lex, this isn't just… It's not just this," he mutters, waving dispassionately at where his leg ends abruptly. "And it's not just Christmas. I-I don't know how to move in this world anymore. In more ways than one."

If he ever did at all. He knows he enjoyed it – he enjoyed being the man with the thrilling, dangerous job and tough, draining hours. Hell, sometimes he thought he was doing good – taking on work that might cost someone else dearly. Mostly he was cocky enough to think no one could do what he was doing.

He believed there couldn't possibly be a better job than the one that his grandfather – his own personal hero and saviour, held for decades. Now he doesn't see how he could've possibly been so blind. How he could have strutted so arrogantly on the surface of a world he barely understood. Now all he sees is blackness taking over the azure ocean. Any fool can understand that – he fucked up. He fucked up the world a little bit and it fucked him up completely. It doesn't sound like a fair trade but he knows better.

He sighs – heavy and defeated, and she scoffs and pulls him up by the hair. It's not painless and his nose almost collides with her chin but then her lips are at the corner of his mouth and her chest bumps his own, and he just closes his eyes and tries to memorize this moment. Let it be bitter – it might also be the last one he spends so close to her and he wants to imprint every little detail on his senses.

"And you think you're the only one?"

He blinks, pulls away. Her pupils are dilated and her lipstick is an absolute mess, disregarding the boundaries of her lips completely, and he no longer takes any delight in the way she scowls at him.

"You think I don't question every step? You think I believed you when you were first flashing me those winning smiles?"

"So now you do?"

She has never been the trusting one, the easily convinced one. It's always a study in preparation and cajoling and, more often than not, a bit of tricking her into things. But once she does feel at home, once she knows she is safe to be herself, once she lets her damn hair down – it's a thing of beauty. He doesn't see how they can continue to work when he can't find his own enthusiasm and inexhaustible energy anymore. He can't bear to have that part of her buried somewhere deep just because he doesn't have the ability to bring it out anymore.

She shrugs as if it's not a big deal whether she does or not. Except they are so close he can feel her tension like it's his own

and he can feel the vibrating force field between them —
gathering, thickening.

"I believe you will never let me pull off my own socks before
bed. I believe you will never let me walk around in your shirt
without bunching it up to check if I'm wearing any underwear
underneath."

He tries and tries and fails not to crave the picture she is
painting, recalling.

"I believe I'm never gonna forget to get you gummy bears,
just like I'll never fail to scold you for eating them. I believe I'm
never gonna let you put on your own sneakers when I'm around
and not because you can't — or whatever bullshit you wanna tell
yourself — but because it makes me feel like you are mine and
mine alone and no one else gets to see you like I do."

He grits his teeth and feels the tears rolling down both sides
of his face, one getting caught between her fingers and making
her press closer still, her inner thighs flush against his own. The
field in between shrinks further, grows denser.

"I believe in us. And if you tell me you don't love me right
now and will never love me again, I—"

Her breath catches and he kisses her cheek even though he
knows he is ruining any chance he might still have of letting her
go. The way his fingers clench her sides, he doesn't know how
much of a chance he had to begin with.

"Well, if you do, I'll leave and — let's face it, I'll probably come
back at New Year's."

He laughs along with her and can't tell which sound is more

choked and disbelieving.

"But… but I believe that you won't. And that I can stay. Period."

"And what of—"

"What? This?"

She leans back and her hand finds its way under the fabric of his sweats and her fingers skim over the raised and unnaturally smooth scarring. It makes him shudder but she just shakes her head – unrelenting, unflinching.

"The world? It will be there when you're ready for it again. When you know what you want to do in it, what you need to do. But right now, I'm here. And I need you to be as well."

"I am."

He responds without thinking and knows in that moment that he never stood a chance against the gravitating power of this woman. When she grins at him – real and elated and believing him, he can't quite remember why he ever wanted to resist. When she leans back into him and he feels her tongue at the roof of his mouth and her hands at the strings of his pants – he can't remember why he hasn't let himself want this. When she pulls away, a strand of her hair stuck to his cheek with the help of their combined tears – he remembers they are a mess but he is past the point of caring.

He is only realizing how much he doesn't want to let her go when she pulls away and slides to the floor. But she takes his pants with her so he aborts his sounds of protest. She looks up, her hand hovering over his scarred flesh – she waits and once again he doesn't really comprehend where this seemingly bottomless well of patience has appeared from. So he just nods and lets her lips cover the flesh she has exposed. For the first time he sees a future in which this is not a big deal to him – the way it isn't a big deal to her even now. It makes him bold.

He pulls her up when he feels her breath on his hipbone and eats away the last of the red on her lips. She seems a bit miffed about the interruption, her hands slide over his chest and there is a purpose to the pinpricks of pain she leaves behind. He just bunches up her silver dress and thinks no memory is worth preserving more than she is worth having.

She – a point of sharp focus in the blur that is the world, the molten core of a planet that is still mostly, blessedly blue, a ball of light stubbornly dispersing the darkness. He thinks – if he is to learn how to move in this world again, he can't think of a better place to start.

11.

The Rabbit Hole

When she was six years old, she walked into The Rabbit Hole Toy Store and to this day it is the greatest disappointment of her life that she managed to walk out perfectly normally afterwards. The Rabbit Hole is a magical place and she expected magical things – an Alice-like adventure on the way back to the land of normality at the very least.

But over the years, she has learnt to see the magic that *is* there.

The large window displays – transformed every week with new, wildly imaginative arrangements (currently, a delicate Snow White figurine fighting a sturdy Santa over the fates of a couple of dwarves and apparently winning).

That one shelf that even the first store manager didn't know the origins of – now serving as a home for a whole kingdom of handcrafted wooden toys (the little frog family has been her favourite from the moment she laid eyes on it).

The toy trains winding their way through spaces unavailable to a mere human; the twinkling lights that are everywhere at all times and yet, somehow, seem to multiply the minute December storms in; the biggest, heaviest and homiest bookshelf she has ever seen that covers the entire back wall of the shop.

The record player in the corner with its ancient collection of Christmas stories, elegant music notes curving over the wall on one side of it and numerous smaller should-be-notes scattered over the other – drawn much less skilfully and in much less aesthetically-pleasing colours (the first time she took her brother to The Rabbit Hole, he added his own masterpiece to the chaotic symphony, then he sat in front of that pile of records and didn't move for an hour).

The fireplace with the enormous pillows in front and the numerous editions of *A Christmas Carol* left open at various chapters (she can see all the kids, laying on their stomachs, feet in the air, reading out loud at different speed until a cacophony of a dozen Scrooges is plaguing the entire store).

The unbelievably charming manager with the sparkling blue eyes and the wild ginger hair and all those freckles, with her booming laugh and her bowties with little teacups on them and her endless collection of striped socks, with her fairytale-inspired puns and the way she sits cross-legged on any available surface and drops down to one knee in front of at least 30 kids a day.

Maya really can't pick a favourite. Or so she tells herself most of the time.

She stops in front of the window display and inspects each toy on the gorgeous fir tree as if she didn't help decorate it a couple of weeks ago. She loves this moment – standing outside, straddling the line between the mundane reality without and the magical world within. She doesn't know if she truly remembers the first time she stepped inside or if she has been told about it so many times that now it feels like her own genuine memory. The human brain – for all its complexities – has always seemed to her ridiculously easy to fool.

But she definitely remembers bouncing so hard she could barely hold on to her mother's hand, skipping ahead after every traffic light and feeling like the red lights lasted for a small eternity. She remembers how in awe she was of the bookshelves towering above her and of the dollhouses that were twice as wide as her 6-year-old self. In her mind, she has a snapshot of her mom – head bent over a book and her chestnut curls catching the soft lighting in the store, making her look like some Arabic princess – paging through heavy tomes, etched with golden letters, in the enormous library of her palace.

She shakes her head and smiles, already planning to drag her mother here after lunch on Friday. She can almost taste the nostalgia on the roof of her mouth – it's sticky and sweet and she knows her mom will love it.

But on top of the carefree childhood memories, tinged with awe for a store that she now knows isn't even that big, have settled some brand new sensations – light and fluttering and inducing the same desire to skip down the street for a whole different reason.

She grabs the cold handle and pushes hard on the heavy door. The buzz of the holiday season rushes at her like a swarm of bees. But she quite likes the buzz in here – it's more of a warm tinkle really, the cheesy Christmas songs mixed with a more non-mainstream selection, the rhythmic roll and drag of the biggest toy train traversing the length of the window, the occasional crack from the fireplace and the triumphant cries of kids who must have spotted just what they were looking for. She stops in the doorway to take it all in and sighs happily as she brushes the snow off the front of her coat and takes off her hat.

Maya has never been a hoarder, she refrains from calling herself a minimalist only to avoid all the expectations and aesthetic obligations attached to the term. It's not that she doesn't like cosy furniture, mountains of pillows, walls covered in posters and cabinets groaning under too many frames, even the occasional – completely useless and sincerely overpriced – trinket from a trip abroad. She just doesn't feel like she has found the place where she wants to accumulate all that crap. Except that she kind of has. So she stands at The Rabbit Hole's entrance and soaks up all the chaos around her.

Until she is spotted. She waves at Tiana, who is manning the register, and ignores her shit-eating grin as she heads for the office in the back – comfortable and familiar enough not to attract any confused looks from staff or customers.

That's where she finds Chrissy Bonvell – manager of The Rabbit Hole.

It will take some time to count all the colours on the woman as it is, but the constant energy that she seems to vibrate with makes that potential task all the more daunting. Even her pacing isn't monotonous. Not with all the unexpected pauses, the halts and starts and false starts, the way she twirls her whole body on the heel of her left boot when she runs out of space in the crowded office or how she throws her head back and shakes it so hard Maya gets some bystander whiplash.

She is as colourful and restless as ever but much less gleeful than Maya can ever remember seeing her.

"No, Armin, I know," she sighs into the phone, cradling it between her head and shoulder just so she can pinch the bridge of her nose, her other hand convulsively pulling at her bowtie. "But perhaps we can wait until after the holidays to— I see. Surprising you don't celebrate."

She rolls her eyes and Maya tries not to laugh at her dry, sarcastic tone. Chrissy twirls around again and that's when she finally spots her in the doorway. She startles for a second before grinning at her – the bright and joyful one she knows.

One might wonder what her deal with Chrissy Bonvell is. And she can't say she has a ready answer but she does have an inkling. It's not entirely unlike that sweet you really, *really* like and you kinda wanna have all the time. But then you try to pace yourself because you're afraid you'll overdo it and get sick of it. Except with a living, breathing, incredibly attractive human being and not a salted caramel brownie. And she's more afraid of Chrissy getting sick of her than the other way around.

After a childhood and an adolescence of daily visits to The Rabbit Hole, after turning 22, Maya decided that it was about time she stopped spending half of her free time in a toy store – no matter how extensive its book and record collections and how comfortable its sofas. She still visited but just the semi-appropriate-for-an-adult amount and she was almost sad to note that she didn't miss it as much as she had expected to.

And then Chrissy happened. To The Rabbit Hole and consequently – to her.

For the past two years, this woman and her toy store have been a treat that Maya allows herself only on weekends. And indiscriminately during the holidays. But she has, honest to Santa, tried not to overdo it. The fact that there are only so many reasons for a 25-year-old to hang out in a toy store might have factored in as well.

Chrissy grins at her and firmly shakes her head when Maya silently offers to leave her to her business.

"Yes, I'm well aware how much the rent will increase from next year," she grits out, turning slightly away from her again, and it is the closest thing to anger she has heard from Chrissy – child (and all human and animal species alike, to be fair) whisperer extraordinaire.

It probably shouldn't send the delicious shiver it does up her spine but what can you do?

"I've got January covered so perhaps we can talk about it at length *next year.*"

Her voice brooks no argument and, sure enough, she finally gets to hang up in the next second. And when she turns to Maya she is all effortless cheer, sparkling eyes and velvety voice once again.

"What brings you to us during the most wonderful time of the year, Miss?"

"A delightful almost-one-year-old whose mother and father have probably gotten him everything he could ever want or need already."

"Ah, the elusive nephew that I have yet to meet."

"I think the almost-one-year-old part kinda explains that."

The other woman hums in what is distinctively not agreement, more like what "I'm humouring you" would sound like, if it were a sound.

"Well, shall we then," she gestures toward the door. "I find almost-one-year-olds particularly challenging to shop for so we'd better get started."

Maya chuckles and takes her sweet time turning around until Chrissy is right beside her, offering her her arm like they're about to walk down a red carpet and not into a holiday madhouse. She doesn't hesitate to take it.

"Armin giving you trouble again?"

"Well, you know, every good tale needs an evil, old warlock or some such."

She laughs – loud and clear, just as they step back into the store and receive a predictable eyebrow wiggle from Tiana.

"And have you already planned a valiant counter-attack?"

"You must have me confused with a charming prince or a pure-hearted princess. I have much more dastardly ideas swirling in my head, toad."

"Terrifying."

"Just you wait and see."

She spends a solid hour lost down The Rabbit Hole –

shopping, if you ask her, procuring the most perfect present for the most perfect little boy – if you ask Chrissy, flirting shamelessly – if you ask Tiana.

They never ask Tiana (but then again, she doesn't wait to be asked).

Two days later, she drags her mom into the place they stumbled upon together all those years ago. She didn't realize how long it's been since her mother was there – watching her rediscover the store is a treat all on its own.

She tries not to be nervous. She tries not to glance at the door behind the cash register every five seconds. She tries not to feel like she is bringing a girl home for the first time – only in reverse because it's actually her mom she has brought and—

Try is the operating word here.

"You know, when you are over ten, you don't have to come with a parent."

If there was ever going to be a moment for her to jump out of her boots like a cartoon character – this would've been it. So that's one less thing to worry about in life, she supposes.

Her mom laughs her honest laugh, not her 'we're neighbours and we need to be on good terms' laugh, so she tries not to glower too much at Chrissy's impish grin.

"Alright," the manager continues. "I might have smuggled a couple of nine-year-olds in the other day. But let's keep that between us."

She wants to roll her eyes, she really does – the woman is

laying it on thick – but her mother seems charmed and Chrissy has been on edge these last few days so she lets her have her fun.

"Where are my manners? Chrissy Bonvell – current manager of this hole."

She sketches a semi-curtsy to go with that and this time Maya does roll her eyes.

"Well, you seem to be good for the place."

Her mom looks around appreciatively before her eyes settle on her and Maya knows it must be a trick of the light but it sure looked like her mother just winked at her.

"Has she shown you her adopted family yet?"

"Her what?"

"Oh, please, allow me."

And, just like that, Chrissy is whisking her mother away, most likely to attempt to humiliate her via her precious frog family. Joke's on her – she feels absolutely no shame over her ridiculous attachment to the wooden amphibians and she makes sure to tell her mother and anyone within earshot just that.

She is down The Rabbit Hole again not three days later, a day before Christmas Eve.

She has her reasons though. Well, if you call bringing the manager a caramel and hazelnut latte at 11 pm a reason. Which she does. So that's that.

She finds her in front of the fireplace – cross-legged on the carpeted floor, leaning against the armchair behind her. Her boots are off, those damn socks are black and purple today and her bowtie has gone with the last customer. The light from the flames is doing wonders for the freckles high on her cheekbones but her brows are pinched together and she has a frankly horrifying amount of papers strewn around her instead of the Christmas books of before.

For a moment, Maya feels like she has just seen Santa with his beard and suit off.

"You should really start locking the door after closing time."

She approaches her from behind and dangles the takeaway cup over her shoulder, watches the tired smile tease the corners of her thin lips and thinks she has wanted few things in life more than to run her hand through Chrissy's hair right now.

Her chuckle is throaty and exhausted.

"Not much to steal here anyway, toad."

She rolls her eyes at the nickname but can't really protest – she willingly makes a fool of herself over those frogs. So instead she plops down beside Chrissy, her knee nudging her thigh, thinks 'go big or go home' and drops her chin on her shoulder.

"I don't know. There's this one record I've been dying to get my hands on."

This time her laugh is a little clearer and she takes a sip of her drink, humming in appreciation.

"I gotta give it to you, you know your Christmas beverages."

She snorts and tips her chin down, digging her nose into Chrissy's shoulder.

"Caramel is the answer to everything."

"So you've told me," she says on a heavy sigh.

"Want me to pour some on that?" she waves her hand at the multitude of documents.

"Afraid *that* is even beyond the powers of caramel."

She sets down her cup, caps her pen and throws it on the pile in obvious disgust.

"Not beyond yours, I hope."

She means it to come out as a joke but her voice catches a little at the very thought of someone other than Chrissy running The Rabbit Hole. The store has been in her life way longer than the woman herself but they are forever intertwined now. She can't imagine having to tear them apart.

Chrissy turns her head so their cheeks brush against each other and Maya can catch the ghost of her grin.

"Fear not. Armin and I have been at each other's throats since I got here. He hasn't got the upper hand yet."

It's flippant but she feels the strength behind it, believes her without needing much proof.

"Enough of this," Chrissy kicks at the papers with those ridiculous black and purple socks and reaches for her hand. "Come on. Let me show you something."

She gets up and pulls her along and Maya lets herself be guided through the store. The warmth and the hum of the madness that is the day before Christmas Eve in a toy store still hang in the air, like invisible festive fireflies. There's a table lamp by the armchair but otherwise the place is only illuminated by twinkling lights and the glow of the fireplace. The numerous shelves create narrow passages and unexpected turns and everything seems even more magical than usual.

She lets the child-like glee play over her face without a second thought, hums and swings their hands between them, much to Chrissy's amusement. She lets her heart be light.

They come to a stop before the shelf of wooden toys and Chrissy lets go of her hand and chuckles, rubbing her thumb over her bottom lip – self-conscious in a way Maya has never seen her before.

"See something new?"

She has lost count of the number of kids she has seen in front of this shelf, looking at the handcrafted wooden figurines with wide, awe-filled eyes. This is the place she will bring anyone who claims that kids don't know quality, that a plastic toy sword is just as good as a hefty wooden one with beautiful carvings on the side. This is the place where she recaptures the wonder that only a child is capable of. The place where she comes when she feels disconnected from that pure child inside her that was always so open to the world and so excited to meet it.

She lets her eyes roam over the familiar toys. The dwarves, sprawled out in hilarious poses, the snowmen, the beautifully realistic Santas and the completely ridiculous ones, the Christmas trees, the spreading oaks and intricate flowers, the exquisite sleighs, the squirrels and bears, the little kittens, the pair of doves, the swan and its little ducklings, the toy soldiers, the princesses with their huge dresses and the simple angel. Her frog family –

the one she hasn't bought because she can't bear to take it away from this place where others fall in love with it every day.

Then she spots them – two frogs she has never seen before: one with a ridiculously oversized bowtie around its neck and the other with a fluffy hat with a goofy star-shaped pompon on top that freakishly resembles the hat stuffed in her coat pocket.

"Did you…" she turns her wide eyes on Chrissy, knowing she rarely does new ones herself since she started running The Rabbit Hole.

"Mhm," she hums and steps closer, her chest bumping Maya's shoulder blade. "Started them in November."

"They—" she looks back at the frogs and reaches out to run one finger over the bowtie. "They are so stinking cute."

Chrissy chuckles behind her – pleased as can be, and her arms come around her waist.

"Can I ask you something?"

"Anything, toad."

"Will you disappear if we walk out of this store?"

She feels Chrissy's snort ruffle the strands of her hair, files away the information that they are literally a breath apart.

"I can assure you I will not. I'm not some ghost, haunting this place and making up for a previous life of Scrooginess."

Maya feels a hand press into her hip and lets herself be turned around so they are facing each other. She watches a pair of blue lights play over Chrissy's forehead, brings her arms around her neck and nods for her to go on.

"I might, however, turn into a frog."

Her eyes are brighter than all the twinkling lights around them and they sparkle twice as teasingly. Maya bites her lip, trying to keep the laughter in, then promptly gives up.

"Good thing I'm really into frogs then."

"I was hoping you'd say that."

12.

New Tales from the New Year

How many women named Alyson Rose can there be in Chicago? He has never been very good at maths. But stubbornness has always come as easy as breathing.

She takes the book out as soon as Ben's door slams behind him. He got an idea on the ride back. He had to write it down right away. So in the wake of her son's excited babbling (wasn't David the best? wasn't he so nice? wasn't he so funny? wasn't he so inspiring? wasn't he so down to earth?) Alyson is free to hug the beautiful tome to her chest, lean against the front door, let out the breath she has been holding longer than it's probably advisable and bang her head on the solid surface behind her.

Yes, as a matter of fact, he is so nice and funny, and inspiring, and down to earth, and annoyingly attractive to boot. And, yes, Alyson is absolutely screwed. She knows it as her fingers clench around the book — the one with those dangerous, tempting numbers inside. She knows it as she drops on the couch in a disgruntled heap. She knows it as she copies every digit into her phone, checking three times that she got it right.

She knows it as she deletes the first of many texts soon to be lost in the void of the unsent.

His mom has her addictions (hello, jalapeños and *Buffy the Vampire Slayer*) but her phone is not one of them. Unless she is working a case, she never has the thing glued to her hand, definitely not when they are spending some „quality mother-son time".

So when she says she is off work until the end of the year, he doesn't understand why she keeps her phone on her at all times. Or why he finds her standing with her fists at her hips, glaring at the device on the kitchen counter as if it demanded to stay up two hours past bedtime.

She doesn't text David Arkwright after meeting him on the 21st of December and she doesn't text him on the 22nd, and she blanches at the very thought of calling him. Now the 23rd is slipping away from her as well and she might be a fucking coward but cowardice and common sense can be shockingly similar in her opinion so whatever.

It's not like this (good lord, *this* isn't even a thing, there's no this or that or anything else, there's just her overprotectiveness of her son, resulting in her stalkerish ways, resulting in a ridiculous borderline-creepy crush, resulting in a proper crush fuelled by this guy's charming ways completely blindsiding her) – it's not like it could ever work.

Despite being on a strict fairytale diet for the last week, she is well-aware that the most *this* can be is a messy and possibly disappointing one-night stand that she cannot afford to have around the holidays. She has a life. She has a son. The whole reason for her predicament, the little shit.

And David… David will hardly be sticking around, if he isn't gone already.

The whole thing is ridiculous and she decides to put it out of her mind, even if she doesn't have the heart to delete his number just yet.

It's the holiday season, a package at her door is confusing but not downright suspicious so she tears into the simple brown wrapping with her patent patience, meaning – none.

Her gasp when she sees the cover of *New Tales from the Old Forest VII* is so loud (and unnecessary dramatic, she scolds herself) she almost ruins the surprise for Ben. She knows that's what it is – a brilliant Christmas gift for her kid – so why can't she sniff out the little twinge of disappointment when the beautiful inscription in Mr Arkwright' ridiculously swirly handwriting is indeed addressed to her son and her son alone?

Ben will be over the moon. So she is over the moon as well. She feels her chest tighten just imagining his face and excitement when he opens this particular present. Then a thick envelope falls from the back of the heavy, leather-bound book, "A. Rose" on it in that same flowy cursive, and she remembers what experiencing that kind of excitement first-hand feels like.

David hasn't done the 'balls of paper lying everywhere but in the trashcan' writer cliché in years. Damn, *years*. He has been writing for years. He is a successful writer. He is a goddamn bestselling author. It still baffles him on occasion.

He doesn't pay much attention to social media, even if he does his best to post something every month or so – a quote, a poem – things that speak to him and he hopes, knows (he is slowly but surely beginning to know), speak to others as well.

But he takes special care of his fan mail. The actual mail. Not many people bother with that these days when their idols or current celeb crushes are just a tweet away. Yet more than David would've thought still do. He has a steady flow of letters, cards and small packages coming his way every month – the perfect amount to remind him that people do want to read his words but not so much that he loses his head.

He has lost his head before and he has no interest in doing it again. But it seems that his heart is the one in danger now, something he never could have predicted, a plot twist so ingenious he has to tip his hat to fate. Alyson Rose is the kind of curveball he could've never seen coming.

If it was just all the different ways that her lips curled when she was amused or impressed, the way her hair kept getting in her eyes and the way they kept flittering away from his when he caught her looking at him, then fine, he wouldn't be in this position right now. But it isn't just her pretty eyes and expressive face. It's the way she cradled his books in her arms and the way she looked when her son seemed to lose the ability to speak. Her son – he has rarely wanted to see what becomes of someone as much as he wants to see what becomes of Ben. Because he knows it's going to be grand. And he wants to help make it happen, he wants to see it happen.

He is absolutely screwed. He knows it as he takes his own brand new copy of *New Tales from the Old Forest VII* off the shelf. He knows it as he lets his pen run with his head and, much more dangerously, with his heart as he dedicates it to the boy whose smile he can still feel tugging up the corners of his own mouth. He knows it as he blows the dust off the typewriter that has so far been only a decorative piece in his office and starts writing to his mother next.

So here he is. Screwed and littering his own house. Because, much as he tries, she refuses to squeeze into a tight corset and twirl at a ball under the gazes of dozens of wish-to-be suitors. Because, much as he tries, he cannot pen anyone smart enough to outsmart her or bright enough to outshine her.

So with one last clumsy ball (he should do this more often, the satisfaction of crumbling paper is almost equal to the frustration of writer's block) he sets all ideas of writing her into a royal world of pomp and glitter aside and pictures the way her eyes flash and change, the way her lips curl and then he unfurls the wings at her back.

And just like that he leaves the ballrooms and castles far behind and the high black mountains and vicious storms ravaging the seas rise up with a roar. He feels himself nodding along as he sprays sea salt on her cheeks, biting his lip as she transforms into wilderness itself and grinning like the fool he is when she soars through the air.

Alyson exercises the one virtue she has never possessed and waits. She wraps Ben's book in the best wrapping paper she has left (and only peaks at the first page, maybe the first five) and, on a whim, ties her own bulky letter with a bow and stuffs both under their tree.

Dinner on Christmas Eve is the kind of cheerful and overindulgent affair that only her son can convince her to create and engage in and as she looks at him eating all the apples and leaving the crust of his pie for last, she knows she will be fine no matter what. And yet... she finds it in herself to admit that maybe just because they are good, doesn't mean they can't be better. Just because it's been the two of them for years, doesn't mean it always has to be.

Later she bites her lip until it almost bleeds but manages to be the adult, the responsible mother, and lets him open one of the presents she got him before bed. No way is he ever falling asleep, if he sees the book. No way is she resisting that letter, if she gives him the book.

Christmas has never let him down!

Ben knows that his mom is humouring him when he starts going on about magic and fate and the power of belief but he also knows that there are some things even she doesn't know. So he humours her in turn and doesn't constantly point out the magic that is so obviously everywhere. But on Christmas he doesn't hold back. And Christmas has always repaid him for his loyalty but this year— This year it outdid itself.

New Tales from the Old Forest VII

VII! As in the one that wouldn't be out for another two months. As in the one no one has seen yet. As in the one he is currently holding in his hands.

The one with David Arkwright's own handwriting inside it, calling him his "favorite fan" and "hopefully future fellow writer" and—

Christmas really outdid itself this year!

She thinks she can't be any more grateful for the absolute joy on her son's face when he tears through the reindeer to get to what she is sure is now his new favourite possession.

Then she realizes Ben's utter fascination with his book also allows her the chance to open her own present in relative peace and privacy. There are the puppy eyes and a beseeching "MOM" and she waves him off, pardoning him for his desire to spend Christmas Day buried in stories she frankly can't wait to read herself. Maybe she has an ulterior motive, maybe there are other things she can't wait to read as well. She thinks she can be forgiven.

Still, she scowls at the way her fingers almost tremble as she rips off the corner of the letter. She is not fancy enough to have a letter opener (this is the first personal letter she has received in literal years) and obviously not sensible enough to keep it together while opening a stupid envelope.

The bulk of the thing should've given it away but she is still surprised, still can't keep in that ridiculous little gasp, when she pulls out the small stack of papers. There are at least twenty pages, typewritten and lightly smudged and wrinkled in places – as if he was figuring out the whole typewriting process along with the story. She doesn't bother hiding in her bedroom, too stunned to think about keeping this from her kid, too busy trying to keep her thoughts from completely running away from her. Her hand is clutching the sheets of paper as if they might decide to slip from her fingers and make a run for it. She takes the couple of steps to the couch, mouth still slightly agape, and plops down in the vacant corner, glancing up to see that she could start setting off fireworks and Ben still wouldn't look up from his book at the other end. She considers getting something to drink but can't bear the thought of those pages anywhere near the damp surface of her kitchen counters. So she just plunges in.

She doesn't call or text him on New Year's.

Because it will be cliché and because he is probably celebrating and because she is too busy watching the fireworks illuminate Ben's wide-eyed, open-mouthed wonder.

And yet. It's only the twelfth minute of 2019 when she thinks of him for the first time this year. And she has a feeling it won't be the last.

On the 18th she drops her exhausted body in the worn-out armchair after doing the dishes and putting her kid to bed. After half a dozen files have already accumulated on her desk. After she changed the leaking faucet in the kitchen and the lightbulb in the hallway that burnt out on the second day of the new year. After she read *New Tales from the Old Forest VII* and read and re-read and re-read and re-read his short story, *her* short story, a dozen times.

She sits down and prays to every deity that isn't still too hungover to listen to her that she hasn't gathered some semblance of courage much too late.

So how is your new year going so far? Alyson Rose (Ben's mom from the signing in NYC)

She re-reads her stupid, stupid text for the eighth time in the last 2 minutes and rolls her eyes at herself for the eighth consecutive time. Maybe she should've also added what she was wearing back then and quoted word for word everything he said. Pathetic. She is so not good at this.

Suddenly it seems like it might be the best one in a good while. David Arkwright (the guy who has been staring a hole in his phone for the last month)

So maybe she is not so bad after all. Maybe it's never too late to start a new story.

ACKNOWLEDGEMENTS

You don't know how crucial this page is until you start trying to publish a book. Some of the stories in here wouldn't be half of what they are, if it wasn't for the input, trained eyes and talented minds of the people who I entrusted them with.

So thank you to Alexander Denkov, Maria Dimkaroska, Maria Todorova, Gergana Rantcheva, my wonderful mother – Nadya Atanasova and whoever my guardian angel is – you are doing amazing.

12. by Lyublyana Atanasova @ Facebook (for everything
to do with this book)
neverlandbohemian @ Instagram (for some poetry)
www.neverlandbohemians.com (for a bit of everything)